An AMISH
Blessing

AN AMISH ROMANCE INSPIRED
BY A BELOVED BIBLE STORY

J.E.B. Spredemann

Published in Indiana by *Blessed Publishing*.

www.jebspredemann.com

All Scripture quotations are taken from the *King James Version* of the *Holy Bible*.

Cover design by iCreate Designs ©
Formatting by Polgarus Studio

ISBN: 978-1-940492-34-6

10 9 8 7 6 5 4 3 2 1

BOOKS BY J.E.B. SPREDEMANN
(*J. Spredemann)

AMISH GIRLS SERIES

Joanna's Struggle
Danika's Journey
Chloe's Revelation
Susanna's Surprise
Annie's Decision
Abigail's Triumph
Brooke's Quest
Leah's Legacy

NOVELS*

*Love Impossible**
*Amish by Accident**
*An Unforgivable Secret** - *Amish Secrets 1*
*A Secret Encounter** - *Amish Secrets 2*
*A Secret of the Heart** - *Amish Secrets 3*
*An Undeniable Secret** - *Amish Secrets 4*
A Secret Sacrifice - *Amish Secrets 5*
*A Secret of the Soul** - *Amish Secrets 6*
*Learning to Love – Saul's Story** (Sequel to Chloe's
Revelation – adult novella)
*Englisch on Purpose (*Prequel to *Amish by Accident)**

NOVELLAS

A Christmas of Mercy – Amish Girls Holiday
*Christmas in Paradise – (*Final book in *Amish by*
Accident trilogy)

NOVELETTES*

Cindy's Story – An Amish Fairly Tale Novelette 1*
Rosabelle's Story – An Amish Fairly Tale Novelette*
2

COMING 2018 (Lord Willing)

An Amish Honor (tentatively Sept-Oct)
A Secret Christmas – Amish Secrets 2.5

Unofficial Glossary
of Pennsylvania Dutch Words

Ach–Oh

Aldi–Girlfriend

Boppli–Baby

Bruder–Brother

Dat, Daed–Dad

Denki–Thanks

Der Herr–The Lord

Die Heilige Schrift–The Holy Script (Sacred Text, Holy Scriptures, German (Luther) Holy Bible)

Dochder–Daughter

Dummkopp–Dummy

Englischer–A non-Amish person

Ferhoodled–Mixed up, Crazy

Fraa–Woman, Wife

Gott–God

Grossmudder - Grandmother

Gut–Good

Jah–Yes

Kinner–Children

Kinskinner–Grandchildren

Lieb (Liebchen)–Love, My Love

Maed–Girls

Mamm–Mom

Nee–No

Ordnung–Rules of the Amish Community
Schatzi–Sweetheart
Vatter–Father

Dear Reader,

This series is loosely based on stories of actual people who are mentioned in the Bible. These books are not necessarily retellings, although you will find quite a bit of similarities between the books and their Bible counterparts. I am, in no way, attempting to rewrite the Bible (God has done a fine job with it and He certainly doesn't need my help!) nor am I depicting the true Biblical characters. The characters in my books are portrayed as Amish and there are some things contained in the actual Biblical accounts that simply cannot be included, due to Amish culture and customs. With that said, I hope that you will enjoy this series as it is, but I also hope that it will encourage you to go back and read the *actual* Bible stories themselves. There are so many truths contained in God's Word that we can never even really scratch the surface of its depth. His mercy and grace are beyond measure.

Blessings,
J. Spredemann

PROLOGUE

Bo King stood on his sweeping porch, gazing out at his fields as he had each morning, a mug of freshly brewed black coffee securely between his hands. He breathed in the delicious aroma of this new blend of coffee beans, as the steam danced before his face and now mingled with the crisp scent of a spring morning.

Der Herr had been so *gut* to him. He had more blessings than any man could ask for. Yet, he lacked one thing. He didn't want to ask God for more—He already knew his heart.

"*Gott*, thank You for Your bountiful blessings. You have given me much. You know my heart and what it longs for, but I will trust You to do what You think is best. Please be by my side on this day which You have created, let me rejoice and be glad in it. Help me to dwell on the blessings that I *do* have and not on that which I don't. Guide my steps and use me to bring joy to others and glory to You. You are my all. Thy will be done. Amen."

He inhaled another breath, sipping on his morning delight. Why had *Gott* allowed him to have that dream last night? What had it meant? It seemed so real. He thought on it now. The images flashed vividly through his mind, his heart…

A woman smiled down at a newborn boppli *in her arms, and gazed into his innocent eyes, as his tiny hand fisted around her loose* kapp *string.*

"I see he has his mamm's *strength," he'd said.*

She looked up into his eyes. The joy and love radiating from her countenance told him this was his wife. Mei fraa.

She surveyed the room, as though searching for someone. "Has the midwife gone?"

"Yes, she left a while ago but she should return shortly. Do you need something? I could get it for you. She ordered me to make sure you get some rest." He lightly massaged her shoulder.

"No, I'm fine."

"Has the little one eaten?" He stared down in wonder at the precious blessing she held.

"He should have a full tummy." She kissed the boppli's *head.*

2

"In that case, he's all mine. You take a nap now, lieb. *You know visitors will be stopping by and you'll need all the energy you can get. Not to mention, this little one will no doubt keep us up at night."* He leaned over and kissed her lips, as though it were the most natural thing in the world, before securing the baby in his arms. Their young son seemed extra tiny next to his own bulky frame.

He'd been grinning so much, the muscles in his face ached.

Even now. Surely he'd been smiling in his sleep.

If only it hadn't been a dream.

Oh, how his heart ached. He understood how Adam must've felt when Creation was nearly complete and he looked around for his perfect match. Only to find none—no one for Adam. Until the Good Lord intervened on his behalf.

Gott, if there's *any* way possible…

ONE

Ruth Johnson peeked out the family room window the moment she heard the Amish buggy rattling down the road. The new Amish family had moved in over a month ago, but she still got a strange thrill each time their buggy drove by.

The situation was peculiar indeed. It seemed odd that an Amish family would purchase the farm next to her family's property. There were no Amish groups nearby, at least, not that she was aware of. She didn't know much about the Amish, but she was pretty sure that they *usually* lived in communities. Had this family distanced themselves from their Amish group on purpose?

She'd grown up on this property in Moab, Indiana and she'd always loved the rolling hills and farms in this area. The land was certainly suitable for the Amish, seeing that they typically grew their own crops. She

was vaguely familiar with the customs of the Amish—
she knew they drove a horse and buggy, dressed
differently, and often farmed the land. Other than that,
she had no clue how they conducted their lives.

This morning, Ruth, her mother, and sisters had
been busy making several batches of chocolate chip
cookies.

"Ruthie, will you take these next door?" Mom
asked.

Heat rose in her cheeks. She'd always been
somewhat timid, so the idea of just showing up on the
doorstep of total strangers did not sound appealing in
the least.

"You want *me* to take them to the neighbors? Can't
Janie go? She's older," Ruth pleaded.

"Only if you're volunteering to do my chores for
me," her sister hollered from the kitchen, where she
currently washed dishes.

That had always been Ruth's least favorite job.
"Never mind, I'll go." She did her best to keep the
begrudging tone out of her reply.

She wasn't about to ask her other sister, Daphne.
She was meaner than an old flustered hornet's nest and
her fury stung twice as hard.

The late morning spring air was absolutely perfect—crisp and lightly scented with the fragrance of wildflowers, especially when the breeze blew softly. Snuggles, Ruth's fluffy calico cat, met her at the door, meowing softly.

"I'm sorry, Snuggles, but these cookies aren't for you. I'm taking them to our new neighbors. Do you want to come with me and meet them too?"

"Meow," was Snuggles' response, as she rubbed her head on Ruth's pant cuff.

"Okay, let's go." She began the quarter-mile trek to their neighbors' farm. About half way there, Snuggles deserted her for a starling that descended from a nearby bush. *So much for company.*

Once Ruth came to the long white pasture fence that separated the two properties, she decided to go around to the front rather than just climb over. A stranger entering their field uninvited might not make the best first impression. She walked down their long driveway and soon spotted a young man clad in suspendered blue pants, a grey buttoned shirt, and a straw hat, whom she guessed must have been one of the family.

As she neared, she became more nervous.

The young man led a horse to a nearby pasture and turned it loose. He met her just as she was about to step onto the porch step. His clothing had obviously experienced much work this morning, evidenced by the stains and unpleasant aroma. She supposed that was to be expected on a working farm.

She stared down at the plate of cookies in her hand to avoid looking at his face. "I brought some cookies."

"I see that." His face brightened and a gentle grin lifted a corner of his mouth.

She finally looked up and found the most gorgeous hazel eyes she'd ever seen. "Oh, I…um…" She felt her cheeks warm. Had the temperature risen on her walk over? "I'm Ruth…uh, Ruthie. Your neighbor."

Oh, but she felt like a fool stumbling over her words.

"*Schee,*" he mumbled.

"What was that?"

He shook his head and smiled. "Nothin'. *Gut* to meet you, neighbor."

Ruth nodded. "You too. What's your name?" She could kick herself for getting flustered.

"Mahlon. Stutzman."

"Oh, I don't think I've heard that name before. Is it an Amish name?"

"*Jah.*" He eyed the plate of cookies.

"Would you like one? They're for your family."

The screen door screeched open and a woman appeared. "Mahlon, do we have a guest?"

He met Ruth's eyes once again and smiled. "*Jah.*"

"Well, why don't you invite her inside?" She chided

and shook her head at Mahlon. She said something to him in a language Ruth couldn't understand.

Mahlon responded with a frown which made Ruth all the more curious what the words had meant.

The woman, whom she presumed to be Mahlon's mother, turned to look at Ruth. "Would you like to come in?"

"Yes, ma'am. Thank you."

Mahlon motioned for her to enter before him.

She walked in and immediately felt warmth. She looked around and spotted a large woodstove near the kitchen. Why on earth did they have a fire this time of the year?

"Come, sit down." The woman motioned to a peculiar-looking rocking chair that appeared to be handmade. It sat next to an identical one in the living room, a small matching table between the two.

Ruth did as told. "My name is Ruth, but most people call me Ruthie. I live next door. My mother asked me to deliver these cookies. We made them this morning."

"Tell your mother thank you, Ruthie." The woman smiled. "I'm Naomi and I'm guessing you've already met Mahlon."

"Yes, we met outside." She glanced at Mahlon as he, too, took a seat in an empty chair. "Don't let me keep you from your work."

"*Nee*. Guests come first." He grinned.

Naomi rose from her chair and disappeared into the kitchen.

Ruth felt like jumping up and running back home as Mahlon eyed her from across the room. A slight smile lifted the corner of his mouth and he winked. Was he flirting with her?

She avoided his handsome gaze, immediately stared at her hands, folded them together, then unfolded them, then rubbed them on her jeans.

Where had Naomi disappeared to? Was it especially dark in there? She glanced up at the ceiling. Where were their light fixtures?

As though reading her mind, Mahlon reached over to a side table and raised the wick on a lantern. The room immediately brightened.

"Lemonade?" Naomi appeared with a tray of glasses and snack bowls.

"Oh, yes, please." She reached for a glass. "Thank you."

"Some popcorn?" Naomi nodded toward the bowls on the tray.

Ruth reached for one. "Thank you." She hadn't expected this hospitality. It was quite refreshing.

Naomi then served Mahlon and set the tray down on the table.

Ruth sipped her lemonade. "This rocking chair is really comfortable. I don't think I've ever seen one like this. Did your husband make it?"

"Mahlon makes and sells them. I make the cushions." Naomi smiled.

"They're very nice, Mahlon. Where do you make them?"

He pointed toward the window. "Just outside in the shop there."

"Do many people buy them?" She'd noticed a small handmade sign out by the road.

"Not yet. But I'm hoping they will sell well here. They were popular with the tourists in Pennsylvania."

"I sometimes work at a furniture store that my uncle owns. I could see if he's interested in selling your rocking chairs."

"Y-you would do that for me?" His humble tone endeared him to her even more.

"Yes, sure. I just need to know a few things. What price you'd sell them to him for…unless you'd rather do consignment. In that case, he'll need to know how much you want out of each one then he'd tack his price onto that. I'll need to know how fast you can make them too."

"How much do you say it would sell for?"

"Oh, I wouldn't know. These are so unique. And I'm

sure they must take some time to make." Ruth ran her hand over one of the chair's arms. "Other rocking chairs in my uncle's store sell for a hundred to a hundred and fifty. I would think you could probably get at least that out of it."

She couldn't read the look on Mahlon's face. Was he pleased or insulted with her assessment? She hoped it wasn't the latter.

"These are really nice. I think people will appreciate the fact that they are homemade and each one is unique—it's sort of like a piece of art." She smiled, hoping Mahlon sensed her admiration for his handiwork.

"Do you think so? That *Englischers* will like them too?"

She frowned. "The English? Oh, I don't know if we get many people visiting from England around here. Besides, it would probably be difficult for them to take the rocking chairs back home, don't you think? Unless, you could ship it for them. But then, I'm thinking that's probably pretty expensive."

Mahlon's grin grew wide as she spoke and he shared a smile with Naomi. Was there some sort of inside joke she didn't get? Or had she said something wrong?

"What? What is it?"

Naomi spoke now. "We call those who are not

Plain—not Amish—*Englischers*."

"Oh, so you would call me *Englischer*, even though I'm not from England?"

"*Jah, Englischer*." Mahlon's eyes sparkled. He was teasing her.

"So, should I call you an *Amisher*?" Ruth returned his jest.

Mahlon laughed out loud.

Ruth looked up at the clock when it chimed. She really should be getting back home. Mom would wonder what happened to her. "I like your clock."

"*Denki*. Eli, my husband, bought that for me as an engagement gift." Naomi smiled.

Ruth glanced at Naomi's hand where a wedding ring would usually adorn a married woman's finger.

Naomi must've notice. "We don't believe in outward adornment. That is why I do not wear a wedding ring like the *Englischers*."

"Oh." Ruth reached for one of her earrings, now feeling self-conscious for wearing them. Not to mention her necklace and ring.

"We don't judge you. That is not our place."

Naomi's statement made her curious now. Did they think that wearing jewelry was sinful?

"I should probably go now." Ruth looked up at the clock again. "Thank you for everything." And she'd truly meant it. Somehow, being here with Naomi and Mahlon just felt right. She didn't feel awkward or out of place like she'd expected to, she felt important, like she'd known them her entire life.

"I could show you my shop before you go." Mahlon offered.

Ruth nodded. "I'd love to see it." She stood up when something caught her eye over in the corner. "That quilt is beautiful."

"*Mamm* made it." Mahlon smiled.

Ruth walked to the quilt draped over one of the chairs. "It's amazing. I wish I could make something like this." She wanted to touch it, to examine it closer.

"I could teach you." Naomi smiled.

"Really? You would? That would be fabulous." Not to mention, she'd get to see Mahlon again.

"I don't have any *dochdern* to teach. I would be happy to. Do you think you could come over on Thursday? I plan to start a new quilt then."

"Thursday would be great." She didn't think her smile could stretch any wider.

Mahlon took his hat off the wall peg and placed it on his head. "Shop's this way."

She didn't miss the warning tone in Naomi's voice as she spoke to Mahlon again in a language Ruth couldn't comprehend. Nor did she miss Mahlon's return grunt. Whatever his mother had spoken to him had not made him happy.

"Goodbye, Naomi. It was a pleasure meeting you."

"Wait." Naomi rushed to the kitchen and returned with a loaf of bread in a clear plastic bag. "For your family."

"Thank you. They will appreciate it. I'll see you Thursday." Ruth took the bread then followed Mahlon outside.

Mahlon walked past a carriage house and into a stately barn. Light filtered in through fiberglass panels on the roof. They passed several empty stalls, which Ruth figured belonged to the horses that now grazed out in the field.

"How many horses do you have?" She noted that the stalls appeared relatively clean and she wondered how often they were mucked out.

"Me? Just one for my courting buggy."

"Oh. But your parents own several?"

"*Jah.* My younger brother Leon has one and *Daed* owns five."

She stopped and peered out one of the openings in the barn. Horses dotted the landscape, grazing on the grass of the rolling hills. Her breath caught at the sheer beauty of the scene. "Which one is yours?"

Mahlon moved next to her and looked out as well. "The palomino."

She looked at him and laughed. "You just spoke a foreign language to me. I know zero about horses."

He smiled and pointed. "See the caramel colored horse with the blond mane and tail? That's mine."

"Oh, she's beautiful."

"He." Mahlon chuckled and Ruth thought the warm sparkle in his eye becoming. He stared down at her and an awkward moment passed.

Suddenly, she was aware of his closeness. She cleared her throat and then stepped away. "We should probably look at your woodshop now."

"*Jah.*" He nodded and then led the way through the barn. At the end was a set of double doors. Mahlon slid the latch and the doors opened to an expansive workspace.

Ruth took in all the tools in the shop and the finished furniture that lined the walls. "Wow! I didn't expect this. Did you make that bedroom set? And the dining room table and chairs?"

"*Daed* and I did."

She walked over to the table and slid her hand over its smooth surface. "Oh, Mahlon, they're beautiful. You do great work."

Pleasure seemed to radiate from his face. "You think so?"

"Yes. It's amazing."

"Thank you for saying that, Ruthie. I like it, but I always wondered if other people thought it was any good."

Ruth's mouth dropped opened. "You mean, no one has ever praised your work before?"

"Praise belongs to *Der Herr,* to God."

"No, I just meant it as a compliment, not worship or anything."

"Oh." He shrugged. "I guess *Mamm* and *Daed* say that I do a *gut* job, but *amazing* and *beautiful* are words I've never heard in reference to my work."

She tapped her chin. "Maybe I should bring my camera over one of these days. That way, I can show my uncle that owns the furniture store. I don't think I've ever seen any handmade items in his store."

"Do you think *Englischers* would like it?"

"Well, I'm an *Englischer* and I like it."

"You're not just saying that? You really mean it?"

Mahlon clearly needed a confidence boost. He was much too humble to see the value of his work. "Yes, I mean it." She pulled her phone out of her pants pocket and glanced down at it to see the time. She'd been there much longer than she'd anticipated. "I should be going now. My mom will wonder why I've been gone this long."

Mahlon nodded and led the way back out of the barn.

"I'll see you on Thursday, then?" She glanced to the house and noticed Naomi peeking through the window.

"If *Der Herr* is willing."

"Bye, Mahlon. Thank you for showing me your shop. And please thank your mom again for the bread."

Mahlon sighed as he watched the beautiful *Englisch* girl walk down his driveway toward her own home. What good fortune to have her as a next-door neighbor. If only she were Amish. If she were, he would have asked to court her.

When she disappeared from sight, he stepped into the house to get another glass of lemonade before continuing his work in the barn.

His mother eyed him as he walked into the kitchen. "It seems like you have taken well to our neighbor."

"She's really nice, ain't so?" *And cute*, he added mentally.

"You must remember that she is *Englisch* and you are not."

"You've already stated that fact, *Mamm*." He wasn't meaning to be disrespectful, but he didn't like being nagged. "We have not joined to any group since we've been here. There is no bishop around to forbid it."

He pulled a pitcher of lemonade from the icebox and poured a glass, then drank nearly the whole thing in one gulp.

"Your father will forbid it." She shook her head. "You need to find a nice Plain girl."

"Like who, *Mamm*? In case you haven't noticed, there isn't exactly an endless supply. The nearest Amish district isn't even within buggy driving distance."

"*Der Herr* will bring someone along. You will see."

He finished his drink and placed the empty glass on the counter. He walked to the door, then turned back to his mother. His eyes met hers. "Perhaps He already has."

Mahlon stepped outside into the sunshine. He looked over toward the neighbors' house and wondered if Ruthie was thinking of him as much as he was thinking of her. He'd thought about kissing her in the barn as they stood so near to each other. He now wondered how she would have reacted if he had done so. Would she have kissed him back or would he have been met with rejection? He hadn't wanted to seem too forward though. The last thing he wanted was to scare her away. *Nee*, he wanted her to return. Often.

Today was shaping up to be a great day, indeed. Mahlon wasn't entirely sure what the future held for him, but if he had anything to do with it, the beautiful neighbor he'd just met would definitely be a part of it.

TWO

$\int$t was finally Thursday. Ruth had been looking forward to this day all week. It seemed like the week had dragged on and on.

She hadn't mentioned much to her family about their new neighbors, except that they were kind. Her parents were thankful for the bread Naomi had sent home with her and she had the note in her hand to prove it.

Her mother seemed pleased that she was going over to the neighbors' to learn how to quilt. She met no resistance from either of her parents. Of course, she hadn't mentioned that she was attracted to Naomi's son. And if she read Mahlon right, he'd been attracted to her as well.

Ruth gathered the bag of walnuts she intended to share with their neighbors. "Mom, I'm going to see Naomi now."

"Okay, be back before dark."

"I will." She looked outside and saw clouds in the distance. It wasn't supposed to rain today, was it? The warm rays of sunshine assured her of a glorious springtime day, but one could never know, as changeable as the Indiana weather could be.

In the space of ten minutes, she was walking up the neighbors' driveway. Mahlon led a team of horses from the barn that were hooked up to some sort of farming implement. Ruth didn't know too much about farming or horses, but she'd always thought horses were beautiful creatures. Perhaps someday Mahlon would teach her how to ride one.

Here she was, getting ahead of herself. Who knows if Mahlon wanted anything to do with her? But he did seem nice. She suspected he was the kind of boy who would teach her to ride if she asked him to.

She lifted a greeting to Mahlon and he waved back. It seemed she wouldn't be conversing with him anytime soon, by the look of it.

Ruth knocked on the door and waited a few seconds before Naomi opened it. The moment the door opened, a rush of warm air caressed her face. She'd have to get used to a warm house if she was to visit this Amish home on a regular basis. Did they use their stove all year round? She cringed at the thought of the sweltering summer months.

"Welcome. Are you ready to make a quilt?"

Ruth shrugged and smiled. It seemed Naomi was much more confident than she was. "I hope so."

"Don't be nervous. You'll get the hang of it in no time. And before you know it, you'll be able to make a quilt on your own without any assistance from me."

Ruth laughed. "I think that will be a long way off."

"We shall see." Naomi smiled and patted her hand, then beckoned her into the kitchen. "Would you like a drink or a snack before we begin?"

"A cold drink would be nice."

While Naomi busied herself in the kitchen, Ruth glanced around the house. It seemed she hadn't had much opportunity to on her last visit. Either that, or her attention had been riveted on Mahlon. As she looked around now though, she noticed how bare the walls were. With the exception of a scenic calendar and a couple of wall lanterns, there were no type of adornments, no photos. But she did notice a china cabinet which seemed to have some type of homemade decorations inside.

"I see you've found the wedding favors. Those were from my cousin's wedding in Pennsylvania."

"Do you have any from your wedding?"

"I do. I kept a couple."

"Do you have a photo album? I'd love to see your

wedding pictures." What had Naomi looked like as a young woman? What did Mahlon look like when he was younger?

"*Ach*, we have no photos. The *Ordnung* forbids them."

"What is the *Ordnung*?"

"It is the rules the Amish live by."

Ruth frowned. "I don't understand. Why would the rules forbid having photos? Especially of one of the most important, if not *the* most important, day of your life?"

"We have memories and mementos. They are sufficient to remember the day."

"But *why* are photographs forbidden?" She tried to imagine a suitable answer but couldn't find one.

"That is something the *Englisch* do. We believe it can become a graven image, something that takes glory away from *Gott*."

She wanted to argue. If that was the case, couldn't anything become a graven image? To her, it seemed like it was a heart problem, not a photo problem.

Instead, Ruth bit her tongue. She still didn't understand, but she didn't want to make Naomi upset with all her questions. It was none of her business what they did anyway.

But for her, she wanted at least a hundred pictures

of her wedding day. She couldn't imagine not having photos to share with her children and grandchildren. But what if she married Mahlon? Would he insist on no photographs?

She wouldn't think of that right now. After all, she and Mahlon had just met. And although she was quite certain they shared a mutual attraction, that didn't mean they had a future together. Maybe she would be wise to steer clear of Mahlon. It was plain to see that their cultural differences clashed too much for them to ever have anything more than friendship together.

"Shall we begin your first lesson?" Naomi entered the room with a cardboard box in her hands. She sat in the chair next to Ruth, set the box down on the table between them, and pulled out a square of fabric. "We'll start with just a simple patch quilt. First, we'll need to cut these pieces of fabric into squares like this one."

Ruth nodded and removed a piece of fabric from the box. That seemed simple enough. "So, we're just cutting a bunch of squares?"

"Yes. Make sure they are all the same size." Naomi handed her a pair of scissors with long sharp blades.

Ruth laid the square on top of the fabric and began cutting. "These cut very well. I don't think I've ever had a pair of scissors that cut like this."

Naomi smiled. "Eli keeps them nice and sharp for me."

"So…tell me what brought your family to Indiana."

"There had been a long drought and we lost all our crops. We heard about the land out here and how everyone was doing so well. Since we didn't have much money and land out here was cheap, we decided it would be best to move. We were up north at first, then we moved here."

"Was it hard to leave your family?"

"My folks had already passed and my siblings had moved away with their families. Many people moved about the same time we did because of the drought." Naomi looked away as though in deep thought. "Eli still has much family there and I have friends that I went to school with. We still write to each other occasionally."

"But there aren't any Amish around here, as far as I know. Don't the Amish usually move to other Amish communities?"

"That's true, we do. I think Eli saw this land and fell in love with it, not realizing how far it was from the nearest Amish district. He's always been a shy-type, though, so I don't think it bothers him as much as it does me."

"You enjoy being around other people, don't you?"

"*Jah*, I miss the fellowship. The ladies would sometimes have frolics."

"What's frolics?"

"A frolic is a get-together. The men sometimes have work frolics too. But the women would get together to can, bake, butcher, make taffy and soap, for sewing and quilting, whenever we had a big job to do. Big tasks are much easier and more fun where there are many people helping."

"Well, we have each other. I could help you do some of those things. I'd love to learn."

Naomi's eyes widened. "You would?"

"Yes. It sounds like fun." Ruth laughed. "Well, except for the butchering. I don't think that would be all that fun. It would probably make me sick."

"For now, we will just concentrate on quilting, *jah*?"

"Yeah." Silence reigned between them as Ruth tried to guess at what Naomi was thinking. She felt bad that this woman had come all this way, leaving her friends and family behind. It was true that she was much younger than Mahlon's mother, but they could still be friends, couldn't they? She longed to help fill the void in Naomi's life. She briefly wondered if Naomi had ever hoped for a daughter.

"*Jah*, it's nice having another female around to talk to." Naomi smiled, opening up a bit more to Ruth. "I'm always around these men, sometimes I forget what it's like to have female company. When Mahlon and Leon

27

marry, their wives will most likely come live with us. Either that, or hopefully they'll live nearby and visit often."

"Do Amish families usually live together?"

"Many times, the youngest son will take over the big house with his family and the aging parents will move to a smaller *dawdi haus*. It is usually connected to the larger home."

"So, when you and Eli get older, you won't be going to a retirement home?"

A look of disapproval briefly crossed Naomi's face, but it was quickly replaced with a gentle smile. "No, Amish care for their own. Our sons and their families will see to our care."

THREE

Mahlon grinned as Ruth stepped out of the house. She had her purse in her hand, but he wasn't ready for her to go. "How did your quilting frolic with *Mamm* go?"

Ruth laughed. "I don't know if I would call it a quilting frolic, but I think it went well. We cut out a bunch of squares and started piecing them together."

Mahlon nodded. "Sounds like you got a *gut* start."

"We did. She wants me to come back next week."

Thunder rumbled overhead and large drops began descending from the sky.

"Oh, no. It looks like I'm going to get drenched." Ruth wiped water from her arm.

"Did you bring an umbrella?"

The wind stirred up and raindrops slapped her face. Her shirt already began to soak through. "No, but I'm not sure how much it would help in this anyway."

Mahlon grasped her hand and pulled her into the shelter of the barn. "*Ach*, that's better." He lifted his straw hat and let the water slide off.

"My mom is expecting me soon, but maybe I should wait out the storm." She worried her lip between her teeth.

"I could take you home in the buggy," he offered. What would it be like to have a *maedel* riding next to him? *Ach*, it would almost seem like they were courting.

"Oh, I wouldn't want you to go through any trouble just for me."

"It's no trouble. Besides, Timber would love a trot in the rain." He moved to take the horse from its stall. "It'll just take me a couple of minutes to hitch him up."

"Thank you, I appreciate it."

A few minutes later, Mahlon lightly smacked the reins on Timber's back, urging him forward. His eyes briefly flitted to the pretty girl beside him.

"This is so much fun." She practically bounced on the buggy seat and her smile stretched wide, making her even more attractive. "I wish it was a clear day so we could see all the farms."

"We can go riding on another day, if you'd like." *Mamm* wouldn't be happy that he'd offered, but he did it just the same.

"That would be great. Mahlon, I really do appreciate the ride."

"It's no problem at all. Anytime." In fact, he wouldn't mind giving her a ride every day.

He pulled up to her driveway. "So this is your place?"

"Yep. Not quite as big as your family's farm."

"It's two story?"

"Yep. My sisters and I all sleep upstairs." She pointed to a window. "That's my room. Our parents' bedroom is downstairs."

"Same with Leon and me. We're both upstairs. I like the view from up high."

"Yeah, me too." She grabbed her things. "I should probably let you go now. Your poor horse is getting all wet."

"He don't mind."

"Oh, I forgot to tell you. I spoke to my uncle yesterday." Her face lit up once again. "Would you be able to go with me into town on Saturday? The weather is supposed to be pleasant the rest of the week. I hope they're right."

"Saturday? What time?" He thought about all of the farm chores that needed to be done.

"Midmorning would probably be best."

"That sounds perfect."

"About nine thirty, then?"

"That should work. I'm taking my dad's truck, so

we can bring along one of your rocking chairs. And if you have any smaller handmade items, we can show those to my uncle too."

Mahlon's spirit soared. A day with this beautiful girl by his side, a ride in a truck, *and* a chance to sell his furniture? It sounded like a dream come true. He'd never been inside an *Englischer's* vehicle without one of his family members riding along too.

"*Denki*, Ruthie."

"Oh, I'm happy to do it. We'll probably stop and get some lunch too, if that's okay with you."

"Lunch sounds *wunderbaar*." He'd have to remember to bring along some money. "If we're in town, *Mamm* might ask me to get some things from the store. Would that be too much trouble?"

"Not at all. I pretty much have the whole day clear, so we can do whatever."

Whatever? Jah, this sounded like a dream come true. Saturday couldn't come soon enough.

"Did you get it all in?"

"*Jah*." He hopped onto the front seat of the truck and slammed the door.

"Easy on the door, Mahlon." Ruth laughed. "My dad will shoot me if I mess up his truck."

"Sorry."

She turned the engine over and shifted into Drive. "I've noticed you're used to slamming doors. Don't your parents ever say anything?"

"*Nee.*" He grinned, his teeth gleaming.

"Well, mine would have a fit." She turned onto the road. "Are you excited?"

"Been looking forward to it since you mentioned it. I didn't get much sleep last night."

Ruth briefly wondered what part of their adventure he was most excited about. She had been looking forward to spending the day with Mahlon and getting to know him better.

"Do you think your uncle will like my furniture? I'm a little nervous."

"I'm sure he will." She glanced his way as she drove around curves and up and down hills. "I thought we'd go there first."

Mahlon blew out a breath.

"You don't need to be nervous. Uncle Jim is really cool." She gave a reassuring smile. "Besides, you do a really good job making your furniture. My uncle would be crazy if he didn't like it."

"I hope you're right." He reached over and briefly

squeezed her hand. "*Denki* for saying that." He looked away.

"I don't think I'll ever understand how y'all think complimenting someone's work is a bad thing. There's nothing prideful about encouragement. Now, I could understand if you went around boasting to everyone. *That*, in my opinion, would be prideful. But just acknowledging a job well done is good and right."

"We are to be humble. Great swelling words lift us up. It should be *Der Herr* who is lifted up, not man." He brandished a smile. "But I do admit that I'm glad you like my work."

"Do you come to town much? I can't imagine you'd take a horse all the way out here."

"We occasionally hire a driver to take us. I mostly stay on the farm. Maybe once a month or every other month, I'll get to go along."

"You don't mind staying on the farm? I think I'd be itching to go places. I can't imagine not being able to just hop in my car and go somewhere if I want to."

"There isn't really a reason for me to go anywhere." He shrugged. "I don't know. I guess I'm kind of a quiet type that doesn't need to be around people all the time. I'm content with what I have."

"That's good." At least his future wife wouldn't have to worry about him running around all the time.

Mahlon beamed as a hundred and fifty dollars burned in his pocket. "I'm so excited, Ruthie! Let's celebrate."

"What do you want to do?"

"How about ice cream?" He grinned.

"Dairy Queen's just up ahead."

"Perfect."

"We'll be eating our dessert before dinner." She smiled. "I knew my uncle would like your work. Do you think you'll be able to keep up with the orders?"

"I hope so. It'll keep me busy for sure."

"You've probably never considered internet orders, huh?"

"*Nee*. But I'll sell my furniture any way I can."

"It's so beautiful down here by the river, isn't it?" Ruth leaned away from the steering wheel and licked her ice cream to keep it from dripping onto her hand.

"*Jah*, it is. This is the first time I've been here." Mahlon pointed to the park and walking trail. "I never knew any of this was here."

"Really?"

"Would you like to go for a walk when we're done eating?" He popped the last of his cone into his mouth and reached for his burger and fries.

"After we're done, I'm going to need to walk." Ruth laughed. How he loved to hear her laugh.

Mahlon bit into his burger and moaned. "*Ach*, this is so good! Ruthie, I think this is one of the best days of my life."

"It doesn't take much to make you happy, does it?" She chuckled.

He shook his head. "No, not really."

About ten minutes later, Ruth wadded up her burger's wrapper and tossed it into the paper bag their food had originally come in. She slid out of the truck and Mahlon followed suit. "Let's go for that walk now?"

"Sure." Mahlon grabbed the paper bag and threw it into the nearest trash receptacle. He reached down and picked up several pieces of trash from the ground near the garbage can. "I hate when people litter."

"Me too."

They walked along the path as a nice breeze swirled fallen leaves from nearby trees at their feet. The sun's rays hit Mahlon's face, sending warmth through his entire body. Or maybe it was being this close to Ruthie that sent warmth through his entire body, he wasn't sure. It was indeed a wonderful *gut* day.

"Should we walk to the bridge and back?"

"Whatever you'd like, Ruthie." Mahlon felt like taking her hand in his own, but the display of public affection went against the ways of his people, so he'd refrain.

Was it sinful to be walking alone with a beautiful young *Englisch* woman? *Jah, it must be*, he told himself. But that didn't change the way he felt about her. He was certain sure he was falling in love with Ruthie. What would *Dat* and *Mamm* say if they knew? He quickly banished the thought. No, he wouldn't think about *Mamm* and *Dat* right now.

"You sure are quiet." Ruth observed.

"Just thinking, is all."

"About what?"

He shrugged. *You*. "The future."

An *Englischer* passed going the opposite direction. "Ruthie?"

Ruth stopped and swirled around. A smile lit up her face. "Brandon!"

The *Englischer* stepped close and engulfed her in a hug, and Mahlon felt his hands clenching at his sides. Who was this Brandon guy?

She stepped back. "How are you? I thought you

were at IU. What are you doing here?"

"I'm down for the summer." He grinned like a fool.

Ruth turned and seemed to finally realize that Mahlon was still standing there. "Brandon, this is Mahlon. He's my neighbor."

The *Englischer* nodded, but Mahlon didn't miss the way he eyed him up and down. He was used to condescending looks from the *Englisch*, but this guy unnerved him.

He quirked an eyebrow. "You're Amish?"

Mahlon nodded once, his stare not leaving the *Englischer's* face.

"Interesting." Brandon looked at Ruth with a questioning gaze, and then back at Mahlon. "Hey, Ruthie, you wanna get together sometime? We can catch up on everything that's been going on since I've been gone." He winked at her.

Was this guy actually asking her for a date while Mahlon was standing right there?

"Sure, Brandon."

Mahlon sighed. This was not good. Not good at all.

"I'll call you. Still got the same number?" He pulled her into another hug.

"Yes, my number's the same."

"See ya."

"Bye." Ruth watched him walk off then turned back

to Mahlon. "Sorry about that."

Mahlon shrugged as though it was of no consequence and frowned. "Who is he?"

"My ex-boyfriend. We broke up before he left for college a year and a half ago."

Mahlon nodded, not sure what to say. But he did know how he felt. Inadequate, inferior, jealous, terrible.

Why should he care, anyway? It wasn't like he and Ruthie stood a chance in the first place. It was right that she should be with someone like that. He realized now he'd just been deceiving himself in thinking that Ruthie might actually be interested in him.

The rest of their walk, shopping trip, and the ride home was shrouded in uncomfortable silence. He almost wished he'd walked home instead.

Ruth pulled up to Mahlon's driveway. "Listen, Mahlon, I'm sorry about Brandon."

He held up a hand to stop her, but he looked away not wanting to see the pained look in her eye. He had enough of his own pain to deal with without Ruthie adding her pity. "*Nee*, it's not you. Goodbye, Ruthie. *Denki* for taking me today."

"Bye."

He didn't turn around as she pulled out of the driveway and onto the road.

Ruth frowned as she pulled into her driveway. She felt like crying. The day with Mahlon had been going so well until they ran into Brandon. It had been so good to see him again. Maybe she shouldn't have agreed to meet with him.

Or maybe she needed to make it clear to Mahlon that she and Brandon were nothing more than friends now. But that would seem too forward, wouldn't it?

Either way, she needed to figure out what went wrong between them and fix it.

She thought on their day and the events that had taken place. Yeah, it was definitely the encounter with Brandon that had him miffed. *So Mahlon was jealous,* Ruth smiled at the thought. He wouldn't have gotten jealous if he didn't care about her.

Mahlon rolled over on his bed and punched his pillow in frustration. Well, he'd *thought* it had been the best day of his life. That was until Mr. Perfect *Englischer* walked into the picture.

Who was he kidding? How could he even think he had a chance with a girl like Ruthie? After all, he was Amish and she…wasn't.

Did he really think she'd want to give up her *Englisch* ways for him? What did he have to offer in comparison to what she already had? It was clear by Mr. Perfect *Englischer* that she could probably get any young man she wanted.

He tossed his pillow on the floor. It was evident that he wouldn't be getting any sleep tonight.

FOUR

It had been almost a week since Ruth had seen Mahlon and she was looking forward to seeing him when she met with Naomi for quilting today.

She combed her mind for an excuse to talk to him and she easily found several. She could mention his furniture and ask if he'd built any new pieces. She could just ask him how he's been lately. Or she could ask him for a favor—this was what she had planned.

Not to mention, she still needed to clear up the incident with Brandon. He'd actually called this week and asked to get together, but she'd declined. She wasn't interested in spending time with Brandon. There was only one young man she wished to spend time with. A certain Amish boy.

She'd seek him out as soon as she and Naomi were finished with their quilting session today.

Mahlon hauled off the remainder of the manure from the horse stalls he'd just mucked out. He proceeded to fill the large wheel barrow with fresh straw, replenishing each stall. He loved the smell of the fresh straw after the barn had been cleaned out. If only it could keep this pleasant aroma.

He distributed the straw into the final stall when Ruth walked into the barn. He'd seen her out of the corner of his eye, longing to go to her but still miffed about her and the *Englisch* guy.

"Hi, Mahlon." Her voice seemed timid, unsure.

He grunted and kept his back to her. The last thing he needed was to gaze into her beautiful eyes.

"Listen, I wanted to talk to you about last week. About Brandon."

He frowned and kept his back to her, continuing to distribute the straw. Very slowly. He huffed.

"Please turn around."

He didn't. "Why?"

"I have something to say to you."

"So say it," he spat out. He knew he was acting like a jerk, but she had been the one to hook up with this Brandon guy.

"Brandon and I aren't seeing each other. We're just friends."

"Yeah, you sure looked like it."

"He called me and I told him that I didn't want to meet with him. I told him I was interested in someone else."

Mahlon sighed and finally turned toward her. "Why are you telling me this?"

She shrugged. "I thought maybe…" She stepped closer to him.

He set the pitchfork against the wall of the stall and stared at her. His eyes searched hers. Was she saying she wanted to date him?

She licked her lips and his gaze flickered toward them.

He stepped close and read the desire in her eyes. She *wanted* him to kiss her. At least, that was what he told himself as he pulled her into his arms and met her lips with his.

It had just been a moment, a delicious moment filled with passion as his lips gently moved on hers, but Mahlon knew in that moment that Ruthie was the one for him.

He reluctantly pulled back for a breath, then brought her close again and deepened the kiss. He wished this moment would never end.

She broke the kiss but seemed reluctant. "I should probably go now."

"Wait." He stared down at his feet, nervous for what his next words would be. He swallowed, gathering his courage. "I need to talk to your brother."

"My brother? I don't have a brother."

"Oh. I see." He scratched his head. "Well then, it wonders me if you'll let me court you."

"Court...? Oh, you mean, you'd like to take me on a date?"

He shrugged. "*Jah*, a date."

"Where would you like to go?"

"Oh, uh, I don't know. Just driving around in my courting buggy, I guess." He frowned. "We could visit in your living room too."

"My living room?"

"Or whatever you want to do."

"I think it might be kind of awkward in my living room. You know, with my parents and sisters there and all."

"Oh." He frowned. "Do they stay up late?"

"Sometimes." She clasped her hands together. "But we could drive around, I guess. That would work."

"Okay, *gut*."

"When would you like to go?"

"Sunday."

"Sunday? Don't you have church or something on Sunday?"

"*Jah*, well, no. Kinda." He blew out a breath. "My folks want to start going, but they'd need to find a driver. The district nearest us is over an hour and a half away."

"That's a long way to go to church. Are there no Amish churches nearby?"

"*Nee*. That's why they haven't made an effort to go until now."

"What changed?"

Mahlon frowned. "They think we should go with the young folks."

"Do you not have any friends here your age?"

"Just you and my brother, Leon. Leon's got some *Englisch* friends that work at the hardware store. But our folks want us to be friends with Plain folk."

"You mean other Amish kids?"

"*Jah*."

"How old are you, Mahlon? I never asked."

"Twenty-one. How old are you?"

"Eighteen. I just graduated high school, so I'm kind of figuring out what I want to do with my life."

"You're my brother's age. He finished school four years ago. After he completed his school, my parents decided it was time to move."

"Wait, four years ago? He finished at fourteen? Is he super smart or something?"

"*Nee*, Amish only believe in attending school until grade eight."

"Wow, I didn't know that." She seemed to be filing facts away in her head. "So, you came to Indiana then?"

"*Jah*. We were up north at first until *Dat* found this property and moved us here. He couldn't pass it up. He and Leon were able to find construction work right away that pays well. *Dat* worked in an indoor factory up north and he never did like it too much. He'd rather be outdoors. *Mamm* isn't too happy that there isn't a *g'may*, an Amish church community, nearby."

"Do you think you'll move again?" He read the worry in her eyes.

"*Nee*. I think *Dat's* feet are firmly planted. This is his dream property, although it still needs a lot of work." He pointed to the ramshackle outbuildings and overgrown foliage. "But it'll keep us busy. I love the large shop for my woodworking tools and since there aren't any Amish bishops around, *Dat* is allowing me to use electric in the shop." He grinned.

"So, if you *do* start going to an Amish church, do you think your parents will expect you to date an Amish girl?"

"They will expect it and hope for it, but it's not up to them."

"Well, I'm happy to go out with you, if you think it will be okay with your parents."

"My folks probably wouldn't approve." He frowned.

"Maybe we shouldn't date, then?"

He thrust his hand through his hair. Was she making excuses not to go out with him? "Did you not like the kiss? Or is it because of that *Englisch* guy?"

"No, of course, I liked the kiss. The kiss was great. And this has nothing to do with Brandon. It's just that if your parents don't approve of me…" She shrugged.

He sighed in relief. "Amish don't usually tell others who they're courting. My folks don't even need to know until we're about to get married." Without an Amish community nearby, who would attend their wedding? He wondered.

"Married?" Her eyes widened.

Maybe he shouldn't have mentioned that just yet. "When the time comes."

"If you're sure about this." He still sensed the hesitance in her voice.

"*Jah*, I am." He took her hand in his.

"Okay, then I guess I'll see you on Sunday. What time?" She briefly looked down at their hands.

"After supper. Is eight okay?"

"Sure. Eight will be fine." She smiled. "I can walk

out and meet you at the end of the driveway. It's probably best if my parents don't know yet."

"I'm looking forward to it." He gazed into her eyes, tempted to kiss her again.

"Yeah, me too."

FIVE

Ruth moved her finger over her lips, remembering Mahlon's kiss from earlier today. It seemed she'd sat dreamy-eyed in her room all evening since dinner had been finished. It was difficult knowing that Mahlon resided just next door.

What was he doing right now? Was he remembering their kisses in the barn too? *She* couldn't seem to get them out of her head. She'd thought of little else since the occurrence.

Mahlon could *kiss*. Better than any other boy she'd dated. Her body quivered at the thought. She could get into all kinds of trouble with a boy, *no, a man* like Mahlon. They'd have to be careful that they didn't get carried away.

Her family had no idea she was smitten with the Amish boy next door. What would Mom and Dad say if they knew? Would they be okay with it? Would they forbid her to see him?

She'd have to keep their relationship a secret. She couldn't chance them forbidding her to visit their next door neighbors. Not just because of Mahlon—he was certainly a huge reason, but also because of Naomi. She'd come to cherish their time together, just the two of them quilting and talking. She was learning much about the Amish culture, things that would be very helpful if she ever became Mahlon's wife.

Mahlon's wife? Yes, that was what she was hoping for. It was true that their Amish culture was vastly different from hers, even a little strange perhaps. But Ruth admired Mahlon's family. Although she'd only met his father and brother once, they seemed amicable.

She couldn't wait to go courting in Mahlon's buggy. The whole idea just seemed romantic. Just the two of them driving around at night with the sound of a horse clip-clopping along the road.

She'd have to sneak out while her parents were watching television or make up some excuse or say she was going to bed early. She'd feel bad about deceiving them, but not as bad as she would feel if she didn't go with Mahlon.

Butterflies danced in her belly as she thought about spending time with the handsome boy next door. Would he kiss her again? She sure hoped so.

Mahlon took his pocket knife from his pocket and began whittling the block of wood he'd brought in from the shop. Perhaps he could carve something nice for Ruthie.

Mamm set her crochet hook down in her lap and looked at *Daed*. "Eli, what do you think of joining the church over in Brighton Township?"

Daed moved his newspaper to the side and rubbed his beard. "That's nearly two hours away by car."

"I know, but it's been so long since we've had fellowship with other Amish. The boys should be going with the young folks, don't you think?"

Mahlon frowned. He was pretty sure this had to do with him spending time with Ruthie.

Daed shrugged. "I suppose."

Mahlon glanced at his brother. If he wasn't mistaken, he was pretty sure that Leon had been interested in an *Englisch* girl as well. He'd snuck out at night more than once, and he'd been dressed nice and smelled of soap. A sure sign he was meeting a *maedel*.

Mahlon stayed quiet, but his brother made his thoughts known. "We don't need to go with the young folks. We have friends."

"But not Amish friends." *Mamm* frowned.

Mahlon understood his mother's unspoken words. She wanted Leon and him to find Amish *maed* to marry and that wouldn't happen where they were now. But even if they did visit another church district, it wasn't like they'd take their buggies along to court any young ladies. They'd have to stay the night over at another family's place and borrow buggies. The whole idea just seemed difficult and awkward to his thinking. If his parents truly wanted them to marry Amish, wouldn't they have settled in an Amish district?

"*Jah*. Peter and I send letters back and forth," Leon said.

Mamm's lips pursed together. "That's not the same thing, is it? See, Eli, that's what I mean."

"If you're wantin' some company, Naomi, why don't you invite that neighbor girl over more often? Ruthie, isn't it?"

Mahlon hid his smile. That sounded just fine to him, although it did sound like delicious torture. He'd be tempted to steal her away to a freshly cleaned horse stall in the barn.

Mamm sighed and turned back to her crocheting, no doubt forfeiting an argument with her introverted husband. "Never mind, Eli."

"We shall be content as we are, *jah*?" *Daed* reached

for his Bible. "Shall we have our evening reading now?"

Mahlon reached for his Bible from the stack that sat on the small table which held the family's most cherished volumes. *Daed* had purchased an English Bible for each of them when they moved away from their Amish district in Northern Indiana. He'd also begun a nightly Bible reading ritual. Mahlon figured *Daed* probably deemed it necessary since they wouldn't be receiving regular spiritual instruction from the Amish leaders. He now wondered if they'd ever join another Amish district.

"Let's continue reading in the book of Romans for the New Testament," *Daed* said. "We left off on chapter three."

Mahlon listened to the words and followed along as *Daed* read the verses. They seemed to paint a pretty pathetic picture of mankind. *Not one person in the entire human race is righteous? Who, then, can be accepted into Heaven?*

Daed continued, but certain parts jumped out at Mahlon. "…the righteousness of God *which is* by faith of Jesus Christ unto all and upon all them that believe…justified freely by his grace through the redemption that is in Christ Jesus…we conclude that a man is justified by faith without the deeds of the law."

Mahlon spoke up. "So all one must do is believe in Jesus Christ and he can receive this grace, God's righteousness?" He looked to *Mamm* and *Daed*.

Mamm glanced at *Daed*, waiting for his explanation.

His father scanned over the verses again. "*Jah*, son. That is what it appears to be saying."

But Mahlon needed more of an explanation, more clarification. "So, let me get this straight. All of mankind is evil. We are without hope. But if we place our trust in Jesus, who was the only one who ever lived on this earth without sin, we will be given God's righteousness and we won't be judged?"

Daed nodded.

Mamm spoke up now. "Yes, Mahlon. You will see when we read the next chapters that this is referring to eternal life. When we trust in Christ's sacrifice on the cross, we allow him to pay our sin debt. He, in turn, gives us eternal life in Heaven."

"This is a gift," *Daed* added. "It's something we cannot earn by our good works."

Mahlon smiled. "That is good news! We only have to believe? What a wonderful *gut* gift!"

"*Jah*, it is." *Mamm* agreed.

Mahlon quietly pondered this newfound truth.

Daed then turned to the book of Ruth for their Old Testament reading, and Mahlon couldn't help but smile. He couldn't help but think about *his* Ruthie. He couldn't help but think about her kisses and their future together.

He was quite certain she was his and they did have a very bright future. After all, she'd told that *Englisch* guy that she wasn't interested. Then she'd proved it to Mahlon by sharing her kisses with him in the barn and agreed to go courting.

Jah, she was his for sure. He was content alright.

SIX

Ruth put on the finishing touches of her makeup and turned in front of the mirror. Would Mahlon like the outfit she'd chosen for their date? Since they'd be driving around and it might get chilly, she'd opted for boots, a pair of dark jeans and a red top. She also grabbed a light hoodie just in case she needed it.

She tiptoed out the back door and hurried down the driveway. The sound of a horse's clip-clop made her smile. Mahlon was almost there.

He pulled slightly into the end of her driveway and slowed the horse to a stop. She noticed how the muscles in his arms moved at just the slightest gesture. She had no doubt that Mahlon was strong and a hard worker.

Before she entered the buggy, she looked up at Mahlon. He seemed fresh, as though he just had a shower. His hair was still wet and slicked back slightly as though he'd run a comb through it, a little falling over his forehead just under his straw hat. He wore a royal blue shirt that brought out the blue in his eyes and nicely defined his physique, with black trousers, and suspenders pressing taut against his chest.

She couldn't take her eyes off him. He was absolutely gorgeous.

He grinned, adding to his attractiveness. "You getting in?"

She cleared her throat. "Oh, uh, yeah."

She felt her cheeks heating as she stepped onto the small buggy step and hoisted herself up. As soon as she did, Mahlon clicked to the horse and set the buggy in motion.

A breeze brought a whiff of something fresh-smelling to her nostrils. She guessed it must've been the soap he'd used. It was quite pleasant compared to when they'd been in the barn after he'd been working all day. Not that she minded the smell of a hardworking man, but she much preferred the freshly-showered scent. She was thankful that he wasn't drenched in cologne like some of the high school boys she'd dated.

"You look nice. Red is a *gut* color for you." Mahlon reached over and took her hand.

"Thank you. You look good too." That was the understatement of the year.

"I'm glad we got some nice weather tonight." He

turned off onto a country road.

"Yeah, me too. It's a perfect evening."

Just then, the horse lifted its tail.

"Hold your breath," Mahlon warned.

Ruth promptly did as told.

The horse's tail resumed its normal position.

"Sorry about Timber's bad manners." He grimaced.

She shrugged. "That's okay, he's an animal. That's what animals do."

"Close your eyes, I have something for you."

She smiled. "I like surprises." She felt him wave a hand in front of her face to be sure her eyes were closed. "They're closed, I promise."

"Well, it's not really a big deal or anything." He put something light into her hand. "You can open them now."

She looked down at the small wood-carved horse in her hand and her mouth hung open. "Mahlon! Did you make this?"

He looked away, uncomfortable with the praise she was heaping on him. "*Jah*."

"This is amazing, Mahlon!" She leaned over and kissed his freshly-shaven cheek. "Thank you."

"So, you like it?"

"Like it? I love it. It's the kindest gift anyone's ever given me." She rubbed her finger over the figurine's smooth surface. "It came from your heart. I'll cherish this for as long as I live."

He stared at her as though he didn't know what to say.

"You are so talented. God has given you great gifts."

"You really think so?"

She nodded.

"*Denki* for saying that, Ruthie."

She held out the small gift, examining it. "I think I'll call him Timber, just like your horse."

Mahlon grinned. "Timber it is."

Mahlon smiled in contentment as he admired the girl at his side. She was so encouraging. Perfect for him in every way, except for the fact that she wasn't Amish. He had no doubt she'd make a *wunderbaar fraa*.

He couldn't believe the excitement she'd exhibited over this small simple gift. In actuality, it held no value. It had just been carved from a piece of discarded wood. But the way Ruthie described it, they way she'd carried on about it…he felt like it was worth a million dollars. He felt like *he* was worth a million dollars. How did she do that to him?

Since they'd met and spent time together, he couldn't imagine his life without her. She was air for his lungs. Nourishment for his soul. The reason he hopped out of bed in the morning. How had he survived before they'd met?

It didn't matter if they went somewhere extravagant or nowhere at all. As long as he had Ruthie by his side, that was all that mattered.

SEVEN

Ruth walked up the lane and Mahlon noticed the quilting stuff in her arms. Before she could reach the door, he called her over.

She glanced at the door then back at him, her look hesitant.

"Ruthie," he whispered loudly, calling her again.

She set her stuff down on the porch swing, then went to meet Mahlon.

He quickly pulled her into one of the fresh barn stalls. No words were needed as he brought her face close and his lips branded to hers. Her back met with the rugged barn wall as his body pressed close. Several minutes passed as the desire between them grew. A pleasurable sound escaped Mahlon's lips and Ruth's heartbeat sped up significantly. She knew they should stop, but…

A noise from the house forced them to jump apart.

It wouldn't do for Mahlon's mother to come out here and find them like this.

Her heartbeat finally began to slow to its natural rhythm as she put distance between them.

"If only we were married…" His hand trailed down her arm and back up again. Longing flashed in his eyes.

"I need to go inside now. Your mom will wonder where I went."

"I know." He shook his head. "*Ach*, I've been looking forward to that all week."

She bit her bottom lip then smiled. "Me too."

He nodded. "Go to *Mamm*, but be sure to come say goodbye before you leave."

"That could be dangerous." She teased.

"Never. I love you, Ruthie."

She gasped. "You do?"

He grinned and nodded. "Ruthie, do you like to fish?"

She laughed at his abrupt change of subject. He seemed to do that a lot. "I don't mind as long as I don't have to bait my hook or clean the fish. That kind of thing makes me squeamish."

"I can do that part if you can fry the fish."

"That part I can do."

"Wonderful *gut*. How does tomorrow sound?"

"I think that would work for me. Are we going in the

buggy or should I drive?" Another buggy ride would certainly be romantic.

"It will take longer in the buggy, but that's not a problem with me." His gaze held that spark of passion she'd come to look forward to.

"How long is the drive?" She tucked her lower lip between her teeth.

"Probably about thirty minutes each way."

"That doesn't sound too bad."

"*Nee*, and it'll give us a chance to talk."

Among other things.

"I think I'd like that." *She* would, but what would her parents say if they knew? And what about *his* mom and dad? But she wouldn't think of that now. Not now, when she had an opportunity to spend more time with this handsome man. *Her* man.

"Then tomorrow it is. What time?"

"Can you be here at nine?" Dad will have left for work by then. It was a good time.

"For sure."

"Do you want me to bring a lunch for us?" Just the two of them, a picnic, and fishing near a quiet stream almost seemed like paradise.

"*Jah*, that sounds perfect." Apparently, Mahlon agreed.

"This looks like a *gut* spot." Mahlon took the quilt he brought and spread it out on the ground a few feet from the water's edge.

Ruth took the picnic basket from the buggy and set it down on the quilt. "Are you hungry yet?"

He smirked and leaned close to her, kissing her lips. "Very." He raised a brow.

She shook her finger at him. "I meant for a snack."

He cocked his head. "A snack, a full meal, dessert. Whatever you've got, Ruthie."

She gasped. "What would your father say if he heard you talking like that?"

"I'm willing to brave his wrath for you."

"We're supposed to be fishing today, remember? I'm sure your mother expects us to bring back some fish for supper."

"If we must." He shook his head in mock disappointment and walked to the buggy to remove their fishing rods. "But for every fish I catch, I want a kiss from you."

She sobered. "Have you talked to your parents about us?"

"No, not yet. Have you talked to yours?"

"I'm too scared to."

"*Jah*. Me too." He grinned.

He took the fishing pole and cast a line into the creek. He settled on the quilt next to Ruth. "I know they won't approve. They will insist I court an Amish girl."

Ruth cast her line in too after Mahlon baited her hook. "I have no idea what my parents will say, but I'm pretty sure they'll have objections too."

"What are we going to do?" His line jiggled and he reeled in a small fish. "I do believe I need a kiss."

"That's too small, you need to throw it back."

"I'll throw it back, but that wasn't the deal."

"Fine." She leaned toward him and lightly pecked his cheek. "There."

"You're looking for a fight, aren't you?"

"Small fish, small kiss."

"Then I'm going to pray my next one is a twenty-pound large-mouth bass."

She laughed. "Are there even bass in this stream?"

He shrugged "I don't know, but I'll pray for one nonetheless."

"What am I gonna do with you?"

"Oh, I have some ideas."

"Like what?" She dared.

"You can start by marrying me. After that, well, whatever we want."

"We haven't even known each other very long. How do you know you're going to be able to put up with me? How do I know if I'm going to be able to put up with you?" She laughed. "Besides, our parents are clueless about our relationship. Good luck getting *them* to consent to our marriage."

"I'm going to tell my folks tonight."

"Really? You're brave."

"Why don't you tell your folks too? We can't hide our relationship forever."

She blew out a breath. "Well, you're right. Sooner or later they'll know. I can hear my father now. *You need to date him for at least two years before you can even consider marriage.*"

"Two years?! That seems like forever." Mahlon shook his head. "You don't think they already suspect something?"

"It's possible. I *have* been spending a lot of time at your place."

"But they think you're meeting with my *mamm.*"

"True. And I *have* been meeting with your mother. But they did know about the two of us going into town together. They may have thought it was strictly business, though."

Mahlon frowned as he remembered the *Englisch* guy again. "Would they rather you marry that *Englischer*?"

"Maybe, but my parents aren't going to choose who I marry. If they don't like the idea of us being together, then maybe we can spend more time with our families as a couple. If they see how we get along, they might just see—"

"That we're perfect for each other?" He grinned and kissed her lips.

"Yes."

EIGHT

"You're what?"

Ruth cringed at her father's raised voice. She attempted to remain calm. "I'm dating Mahlon, our neighbor."

"The Amish boy?" Her mother's voice screeched.

"Yes, he's Amish. He's twenty-one years old. He owns his own woodshop and does great work. You should see his furniture. Uncle Jim is carrying some in his store." She felt like she was trying to sell him.

Her father frowned. "But he's Amish."

She held out her hands, palms up. "What is wrong with that?"

"Really, Ruthie? You have to ask?" Her father shook his head. "They don't even drive automobiles or use tractors. It's like they're stuck in the nineteenth century or something."

"What if he decides he wants to marry you?" Her

mother spoke up. "Do you plan to wear one of those strange bonnets and wear homemade dresses your entire life? Ruthie, you really need to think about this. Making quilts with his mother is one thing, but this is an entirely different matter."

"Ruthie, it takes more than just kissing to make a relationship work." Was her dad really saying this?

"I know that, Dad."

"You *say* you do, but I think you have a fairy tale in your head, not reality. You're only eighteen, Ruthie."

"That's right. What about college?" Her mother added.

Ruth sighed. "I don't care about college."

"Since when?" Her mom frowned. "This is the first I've heard of it."

She wanted to say that Mahlon hadn't even needed to go to high school, but somehow she didn't think that was going to help their plight.

Her mom continued. "I thought you wanted to take those computer courses. Do the Amish even use computers?"

"No." She swallowed.

"They don't even use electricity, June." Her father scoffed. "You need to *stop* seeing that Amish boy, starting now."

"What?" Tears pricked her eyes. "No."

"The sooner you break things off, the easier it will be for both of you."

"Dad, no. It's *my* life."

"You're making a terrible decision, honey," her mother said. "You come from two different worlds."

"You will not defy me, Ruth. You don't know what you're doing. I hate to do this, but I *have* to put my foot down here. If you plan to stay living under *this* roof, you *will* break things off with him." Her dad wasn't going to budge.

"And it's probably a good idea if you didn't go over there anymore." Her mom added.

She wanted to protest. She wanted to tell them how she was nearly finished with her quilt and how she planned to help Naomi with canning this summer. But none of that would matter to her parents. They didn't care about what *she* wanted.

"I want you to enroll in college for next semester. You can choose whether you want to go to junior college or to the university."

"I told you I don't want to go to college!" She pushed away her tears and rushed to her bedroom.

How on earth was she going to tell Mahlon that their relationship was over? Would her father really kick her out if she continued to see him? She'd consider moving out if she had enough money to support herself, but she didn't. Her job at her uncle's furniture store was enough to keep gas in her tank, pay for her insurance, and have some extra spending money, but it would never provide enough for rent.

She opened her drawer and took out the small horse Mahlon had carved with his own two hands and given her as a gift. He'd been so thoughtful, so caring. He was a good man. The kind of man a woman ought to marry.

The truth was she loved Mahlon and she couldn't see herself marrying anyone else. Maybe she was dreaming, maybe it was just a fairy tale.

But she didn't care about having a television or not being able to use her computer. Those things weren't important to her in the least. She could learn to sew and bake and make her own soap…as a matter of fact, she looked forward to learning these things. She looked forward to having a quiet time with just family around, of sharing meals together, of bonding. This was the life she wanted—a plain and simple life with Mahlon as her husband…someday.

Ruth reached for the door handle.

"Where are you going, Ruthie?"

She turned around at her father's question. "I need to go talk to Mahlon."

"There's no need to do that. I plan to go talk to him today."

Ruth's mouth gaped open. "You won't even let me talk to him?"

"It's not a good idea. It's better this way. You'll understand someday when you've gained a little more wisdom."

"Really, Dad?" *Unbelievable.* She'd been too stunned to even argue with him.

She took a deep breath and calmed herself. *It's okay, this is just temporary. Dad is upset right now and probably a little shocked. He'll get over it soon.* She hoped with all her heart that she was right, because if she wasn't…

No, she wouldn't think about that right now. There was *no way* she was losing Mahlon—the best guy she'd ever known—forever.

The crunch of rubber tires against the gravel driveway unmistakably told Mahlon that an *Englischer* had come to visit.

His heart sped up and he quickened his step. He hoped it was Ruthie. He'd been thinking of little else since their fishing excursion yesterday.

He sauntered out of the barn, a grin lighting his face, then slowed his steps as he realized the vehicle wasn't hers. He frowned. It definitely wasn't Ruthie, he realized, as an *Englisch* man near his folks' age exited the vehicle.

The man walked toward him with purposeful steps. "Are you Mahlon?"

He nodded. "*Jah.*" Who was this man and how did he know his name?

"I'm Ruthie's father." Usually, *Englischers* would extend a friendly hand to shake. Not this man.

Mahlon cleared his throat and stood erect. "*Gut* to meet you."

The man disregarded his greeting. "I understand you and my daughter have been dating. That needs to stop."

Mahlon frowned. Was he saying Ruthie was no longer allowed to see him?

"Ruthie won't be coming over here anymore. Not to quilt with your mother, and not to see you. And I don't want you trying to contact her either."

"Why?"

"You come from two very different worlds. I don't think I need to explain that to you, do I?"

Mahlon shook his head but remained silent, trying to process this man's words.

"My daughter is not cut out for an Amish life, and her mother and I want what's best for her. She's signing up for college in the fall and we don't want her to be distracted from her studies. Do you understand?" Her father's eyes narrowed and zeroed in on his.

"*Jah*, I understand but I don't agree."

"Mahlon, let me be frank. You don't need to agree, this isn't a request. I realize my daughter is beautiful. You are a young man and I know what men your age want. You won't get that from my daughter."

His hands clenched at his sides. "I care for Ruthie and I want what's best for her too. I'm not going to take advantage of her. She means a lot to me."

"If that's *true*, then you'll do as I've asked. I have no respect for someone who can't honor my wishes, especially when it concerns one of my daughters."

"When may I see her then?"

"I'd rather you didn't."

"Ever?" Mahlon frowned. "If I were an *Englischer*, would you be saying the same thing to me?"

"*If* you were, as you call it, an *Englischer* and an acceptable possible mate, I'd tell you to contact my daughter when she's finished with her schooling. That would be in about four years at the soonest. But she'll most likely want to pursue a career after she's completed her studies, so it will probably be longer.

"But that doesn't really matter, though, does it? You're Amish, not *Englisch*, and I'm suspecting that's what you'll *always* be. I hate to break it you, but my daughter has higher aspirations than to wait on a man hand and foot her whole life."

As Mahlon's fists clenched tight at his side, the slivers of nails cut into his skin. He didn't miss the hint of superiority, nor the condescension in this man's voice.

Did this man put no value on a wife and a mother? Surely a woman's greatest blessing was to guide her household and teach her children the ways of the Lord, wasn't it? There was certainly no shame in it, as this man made it sound. *Nee*, it was a true honor and the highest of callings. Had he never heard that the hand that rocked the cradle was the one that ruled the world?

Four years at the soonest? Mahlon felt as though the wind had been knocked out of him. Waiting four years would be torture. And Ruthie's father was right about one thing. He *would* always be Amish. Was it unfair to Ruthie to ask her to give up her *Englisch* life for him? Maybe her father was right…but even if he was, it didn't make the sting of losing his sweetheart hurt any less.

NINE

Seeing her beloved across the field riding his horse, equated to torture of the worst kind. He was just next door, yet she couldn't speak to him. He was just next door, yet she couldn't gaze into his eyes. He was just next door, yet she couldn't walk into his arms, feel his lips on hers, communicate her love for him.

Pure torture. That was exactly what it was. And it was all so unjust.

She pulled out the wooden horse Mahlon had carved from her pocket. She'd kept it there as a reminder of him. As she studied it, she remembered when Mahlon had given it to her. He'd been so shy and hesitant, unsure whether she would appreciate it or not. How could she *not* appreciate such a thoughtful gift? She now wondered if this small gift, Timber, would be all she had to remember their romance by.

Ruth hated the fact that she'd been watched like a

hawk the last couple of weeks, ever since her father discovered her and Mahlon's courtship. She never should have said a thing. They should have just kept their entire courtship a secret until they decided to get married. But it was too late for that now.

She felt like a prisoner in her own home. She needed to find a way to get in contact with Mahlon, but she wasn't sure how she could do it without raising suspicions in her parents' minds.

An idea suddenly came to her. What if she wrote him a letter? She could send it off through the mail when she went to work and her parents would never know. But what about his parents? Would they allow him to read a letter from her? She'd have to take that chance.

She opened up her desk drawer and found a notebook and pen. Just in case his parents had any suspicions, she'd need to be cryptic. Hopefully, Mahlon was good at picking up on hints.

Dear Mahlon,

Hi. I hope you and your family are doing well. Did your mother finish her quilt yet? I'd love to see it one day.

My uncle was able to sell your rocking chair. Do you think you'd be able to drop off a couple more for him this week? Sorry, I'll be

*working so I won't be able to give you a ride.
You'll need to hire a driver.*

*I'm working more hours at the store and
my parents signed me up for college in the fall,
so we probably won't be seeing very much of
each other.*

Tell Timber I miss him.

Ruthie

Not seeing Ruth the last few weeks, and believing he
might never see her again, nearly sent Mahlon into
depression. He been moping around, very unlike
himself. Somehow, though, he'd been inspired when
working in the woodshop. It must've been Ruthie's
words of encouragement that had been echoing in his
mind.

He'd been trying to find a way to contact Ruthie, but
it seemed like she was never home alone. He'd watched
her house from his bedroom window through
binoculars, attempting to figure out a time when her
folks would be gone, to no avail.

When he checked the mail today, his heart soared to
see a letter from Ruthie. He'd received, what seemed to
be, an answer to his prayer.

Mahlon reread the letter. *This* was his chance to see Ruthie! If he could get a ride into town alone, he could be dropped off at the furniture store and deliver his rocking chairs. Ruthie would probably be working, so it was the perfect opportunity. They wouldn't have a lot of time together, but it would be better than nothing.

Ruth's mood brightened when she looked up from her desk in the furniture showroom. She paged her uncle's office. "Uncle Jim, Mahlon's here with some of those rocking chairs."

"Great. I'll be right there. I'm finishing up some paperwork. Will you greet him and show him a seat, please?"

"Sure." She walked to the entrance, just as Mahlon opened the door. His driver was with him.

He turned to the man. "I'll unload those, then you can go. Would you mind picking me up in an hour and a half?"

His driver nodded. "Sure."

Ruth ached to jump into Mahlon's arms and tell him how much she'd missed him, but to do so now would be inappropriate. She needed to remain professional.

She couldn't chance getting caught with Mahlon and her uncle reporting back to her father.

"Mahlon, you may go ahead and bring the chairs into the showroom. When my uncle comes out, he'll let you know exactly where he wants them."

He nodded, an uneasy look on his face.

She leaned forward and lowered her voice. "Will you have lunch with me today?"

His grin spread wide. "I'd love to."

"I'm hoping that my dad will eventually cool off and let me see you." Ruth drummed her fingers on the steering wheel.

Mahlon frowned. "I don't think that's going to happen. He was pretty serious when he came to talk to me. I think he hates me. He doesn't want you anywhere near me."

"I don't know how he thinks he can control my life." She brushed away a tear. "Do you know what he told me?"

Mahlon shook his head, aching to pull her close.

"He said he was going to kick me out of the house if I kept seeing you against his wishes. How can he even do that?" She parked the car facing the river. It was the same spot they'd visited before.

"I can't believe he would say that. Do you think he really would?"

"I don't know." She blew out a breath. "But I don't want to find out. What would I do then?"

"I don't know." His face brightened. "You'd have to come live with me."

She shook her head and lifted a half smile. "And you think your parents would approve of that?"

"*Nee.*" He winked. "We could sneak you in."

"What are we going to do?"

"I think I'm going to kiss you right now."

She blinked, then smiled shyly. "Okay."

Ruth couldn't wipe the silly grin off her face as she watched Mahlon ride off with his driver. They hadn't solved any of their problems, but at least they'd gotten to see each other. She already knew that she had missed him, but now she realized just how much.

Her uncle was about to walk past her desk when he suddenly stopped and turned to her. "Oh, Ruthie, I nearly forgot. Your father called while you were out."

The hairs on her arms stood like soldiers at attention. "He did? What did you say?"

"That you were out to lunch with Mahlon."

No, no, no! And now she had no way to contact Mahlon to warn him.

"Did he say what he wanted?"

Uncle Jim shook his head. "He just said that he'd talk to you when you got home."

That was the last place she was looking forward to going to today.

I'm sorry, Mahlon.

TEN

"Did you see my daughter today?" Ruthie's father stood in front of Mahlon, demanding an answer. He'd shown up shortly after Mahlon returned from town.

"*Jah*, at the furniture shop when I dropped off the rocking chairs."

"And you *also* had lunch together, am I correct?" The red in Ruthie's *daed*'s face clearly revealed his lividity to Mahlon.

Mahlon nodded. His goose was cooked. How had he found them out? Had Ruthie's father been stalking him?

"Did you have any *physical* contact with my daughter?"

"Physical contact?" Mahlon swallowed.

"Let me be specific." He didn't mince his words. "Did you hold her hand, hug her, kiss her, or anything else that would encompass *touching* my daughter?"

He'd done all three. "*Jah.*" He nodded.

"Where are your parents?" The man requested. No, demanded.

"*Dat* is in the barn and *Mamm* is cooking supper."

"I'd like to speak with *both* of them."

Oh, no. This wasn't *gut* at all.

"I will get *Dat.*" He left Ruthie's father standing in the driveway and slowly made his way into the darkened barn. *Dat* was mending a harness. His father detested being interrupted while he was working, but this situation was beyond his control.

"Ruthie's father would like to talk to you and *Mamm.*" Mahlon released a heavy sigh. This would not turn out well for him.

"What's this about, *sohn*?" *Dat* frowned and his eyes bored into Mahlon's. How was it that his father could sense when trouble was brewing?

"Her *vatter* doesn't want us to see each other."

"*Jah*, I know that much."

He couldn't bring himself to lift his eyes to his father's. "We did."

His father nodded, and disappointment marked his face. Mahlon hated that look. He brushed past Mahlon with a heavy sigh and marched out of the barn without a word.

Mahlon walked out behind him, knowing he'd need to be present for the reprimand as well.

Ruthie's father nodded to *Dat*. "I apologize for distracting you from your work, but this can't wait. Is your wife here? I'd like her to hear what I have to say as well."

"*Jah*. We can go inside." *Dat* suggested and led the way.

Mahlon fell in line behind Ruthie's father, dread filling his gut.

Dat called *Mamm* into the sitting area and the four of them stood there in awkward silence before Ruthie's father spoke up. "A few weeks ago, I came by and asked Mahlon to discontinue his relationship with my daughter. He assured me that he would."

Mahlon wanted to object. He wanted to speak up and say that he never agreed to it. He'd never been given a choice. But interrupting his elders would be frowned upon and he couldn't afford for *Dat's* anger to kindle more than it already had.

"I think you can agree that a relationship between the two of them would never work."

Ruthie's father waited for his folks to agree.

He continued. "If Mahlon continues to disrespect me by disregarding my wishes, I will have no choice but to file a restraining order against him."

"What does this mean?" *Dat* asked Ruthie's father.

"It is a legal document that would forbid Mahlon to come into contact with my daughter. If he violates the edict and comes near Ruthie, he will be arrested and go to jail."

"You would have Mahlon *arrested* for speaking to Ruthie?" Mahlon heard the anguish in his mother's voice.

"This is just a warning. It's Mahlon's second chance. I'm not filing the restraining order *yet*. But if I see or hear or find out that they continue to have contact, then yes, I *will* file the restraining order. A father has a right to protect his daughter."

Pain clenched Mahlon's heart. He could hold his silence no longer. "Ruthie doesn't need to be *protected* from me. I would never hurt her!"

"Mahlon, *nee*." His father warned. *Dat* turned to Ruthie's father. "He will do as you say."

Mahlon turned around and stomped off in search of Timber. He needed to ride right now. He had to get away from there—away from the ones trying to sabotage his life, away from the ones attempting to destroy his future, away from the ones ruining his chance at happiness.

What would he do without Ruthie in his life? She'd become his everything.

He thought he'd missed her before, but after holding her in his arms today, he knew there was no way he could stay away from her. He had to find a way. They *loved* each other. No one should have a right to interfere with that. Not his parents, not her parents, and certainly not the law. *No one.*

He didn't know what his next course of action would be, but he *had* to do something.

ELEVEN

If this plan didn't work, he'd be in deep trouble of the worst kind. If this plan didn't work, it could be the last time he ever saw his beloved. If this plan didn't work, he could very well find himself sitting in a jail cell.

There was much at stake, and Mahlon hadn't failed to realize that. But he couldn't just cut ties with Ruthie without saying goodbye. She needed to know how he felt about her.

He'd have to be careful, but she was worth the risk. He could only hope Ruthie's family weren't light sleepers.

He'd waited until the house had been quiet for some time before executing his plan. Ruthie's light was still on so he knew she'd be awake.

Praise God her family didn't own a dog.

He blew out an anxious breath and tossed the tiny pebble, then hid behind a bush. It barely clinked against her window, so he was unsure if she'd heard it. He waited in silence.

Something suddenly brushed up against his leg and he nearly jumped out of his skin. He bit his tongue to keep from expressing his startlement. It was only a cat, he realized with a relieved breath.

Ruthie's light went out and he quickly peeked from behind the bush. He saw her squinting through the window, searching the yard, and he waved. She slowly pushed the window up.

Mahlon put a finger to his lips so she wouldn't speak. He held up a scrap of paper to show her, crumpled it up, and then placed it inside one of the bushes in her yard.

Ruthie nodded and a sad smile lifted at one corner of her mouth. Oh, how he longed to make her happy!

He placed his hand over his mouth and blew her a kiss. She did the same. He gazed at her momentarily, cementing her image in his mind, before he disappeared into the night.

As soon as Ruth had a free moment when she wasn't being watched like a hawk, she went outside pretending to be searching for the cat. She called out to Snuggles several times once she came near the bush Mahlon had hid behind the prior evening. She moved around the bush, retrieved his note and subtly stuffed it into her pocket. She picked up Snuggles, petted him for a few moments, then hurried to her room to read what Mahlon had written.

It wasn't a note at all, she discovered, but some kind of code. She guessed he was trying to be vague in case her father or someone else found the note. Anyone would have thought it was just a piece of trash by looking at it. Mahlon was clever. She could only hope she fully understood the note's meaning.

She examined the letters on the crumpled note: TH5RIV. Was it a license plate number? No. The five rivers? Or was the five an S? No, she studied it again. *Mahlon, what does this mean?* She whispered internally, as though she could summon his thoughts. *Wait.* TH-Thursday? 5-at five o'clock. RIV-by the river. Yes, that had to be it! He wanted her to meet him on Thursday, at five, by the river.

Thursday was tomorrow. It was just after work, so Dad wouldn't call during lunch time, and if he did, she'd be there. It was perfect. No one would suspect a thing.

Mahlon sat on a bench, looking out at the Ohio River. Would this be the last time he and Ruthie saw each other? He couldn't abide the thought.

This wasn't fair. None of it. Why couldn't they just love each other without other people interfering? They were adults and plenty smart enough to make their own decisions. At least, to Mahlon's thinking.

He understood that their parents had concerns, and there was nothing wrong with that. But instead of forcing their will upon them, why couldn't they voice their concerns and let Mahlon and Ruthie make the final decision? After all, it was their lives. *Their* future.

Wouldn't *Gott's* will be done anyway? He thought about that for a moment. No, *Gott's* will wasn't always done. Sometimes, *many* times, people did things contrary to *Gott's* will. And *Gott*, unlike Ruthie's father, didn't force His will on others. He delineated His will in His Word, and allowed His children to *choose* whether they would follow it or not. But He *never* forced them to obey.

He recalled one time when he'd been riding in an *Englischer's* car. The man had been listening to some type of sermon, it seemed. At the time, he hadn't been paying much attention, but now one phrase floated back to his mind. *You can choose to go to Hell, if you want to.* The thought had seemed absurd to him, but the truth of it remained. Heaven was available for all. God gave each person a *choice*.

That's all he wanted from their folks – the chance to *choose* their own path.

He bowed his head. *Gott, if it is Your will that Ruthie and I be together, please make a way. I know her father doesn't like me and I don't know why. You know that I love her. I would like to have her as my wife. I will do my best to lead her in the way You have shown me according to Your Word. Please guide me and show me a clear path. Amen.*

Just as he lifted his head, he saw Ruthie's vehicle pull into one of the parking places. He went to meet her.

"Hop in. Let's talk in my car."

He did as she suggested.

"Hi." He wanted to lean over and give her a kiss, but he refrained.

"Mahlon, my parents keep talking about sending me off to a university." Tears pricked her eyes. "I don't want to be away from you."

"What can we do?"

"I don't know." She sniffled and he reached up and wiped the tears from her cheeks with his thumbs. How he hated to see her cry.

"I want to marry you, Ruthie, I'm sure of it. But I'm afraid our folks are not going to approve. Ever."

"I had a feeling your parents didn't really like me either." She touched his hand.

"*Nee*, that's not it. I think they *do* like you. It's just because I'm Amish and you're not. They want me to marry a Plain girl."

"I know. My parents feel the same way."

"Your father told me as much."

"What did he say?" She grimaced.

"To stay away from you. Basically, because I'm Amish and you're *Englisch,* it would never work between us." He shrugged. "But *I* think it can work. I love you, Ruthie, and I want to marry you someday. Do you feel the same way?"

"Yes, of course. I just wish we had more time to spend together getting to know each other. It's not fair that our parents won't let us date anymore."

"Your father said he would send me to jail if he finds out we've been seeing each other."

"What? He can't send you to jail, can he?"

"He said something about an order. I'm not sure what it's called."

Ruthie shook her head. "A restraining order. I cannot believe it! He threatened you with a restraining order? Oh, that makes me mad."

"What are we going to do?"

"We could always elope."

"I don't know what that is."

"We're both over eighteen, which means we're adults. We can go get married in a private ceremony and no one can say anything. Once it's done, it's done."

"You… you would *want* to do this?"

"Not really." She frowned. "I've always dreamed of having a big wedding and wearing a beautiful white wedding dress. But if this is the only way I can marry you, then I'd be happy to do it. I love you, Mahlon, and I can't imagine being married to anybody else."

Mahlon swallowed and wiped his sweaty hands on his trousers. "I'll buy you a fancy dress. I want you to at least have that."

She reached over and squeezed his hand, excitement shining in her eyes. His heart was surely beating double-time. Were they really contemplating this?

"Okay, let's think about this a minute." She whipped out her phone and looked up 'Marriage License in Indiana.' She read the list. "We'll need IDs. I have my driver's license. Do *you* have any type of ID?"

"I can sneak my birth certificate from *Dat's* file."

"That should work." She nodded.

"Do you have a piece of mail addressed to you? A bank statement or something?"

He thought for a moment of the drawer in his bureau where he kept his important mail. "*Jah*, I think so."

"Okay, bring that. We'll need money too. I have a little."

"I have plenty. Don't worry about that." He rubbed the top her hand with his thumb.

"We might be gone for a few days."

"A few days?" Confusion splashed across his face.

"I think I read somewhere that a contract can be contested for up to three days. In case our parents try to force us to get an annulment, I think it would be best if we left town for a few days." She smiled. "It could be our honeymoon."

His eyes met hers. Could she read the apprehension in them? And the excitement? "*Jah*, that sounds *gut*."

"I'm nervous." She laughed.

"*Jah*, me too. When do you want to do this?"

"Soon, or I might lose my nerve."

"Are you for *sure* you want to do this?"

She nodded. "I've never been more sure about anything in my life. And Mahlon?" She kissed him. "I don't need a fancy dress. Just marrying you will be enough."

"Okay, when?"

"Tomorrow. I'll leave for work in the morning like I always do. You can meet me at the end of your driveway. Be sure you have your birth certificate and bank statement and some extra clothes. Remember, we'll be gone a few days at least." She blew out a breath. "We can leave a note for our parents so they won't worry too much. We'll be vague about it. I'd rather not tell them about the wedding until we return. That way, my dad won't know where to track us down. They won't be happy about it *at all*, but at least they won't think we're dead or that we've been kidnapped." She chuckled nervously.

"Tomorrow, then. What time?"

"I'll pick you up about eight thirty. The clerk's office should be open by the time we get there, but I don't know how long it will take for them to marry us. I'm glad they don't have a waiting period."

"What about your car? Won't your folks be able to find us? What if they call the police?"

"My car is registered in my own name, so I don't think that will be a problem. The note should be enough to tell the police that we left together voluntarily. If we get stopped, I think the police will be on our side since we are both adults." She lifted a nervous smile. "Where would you like to go for our honeymoon?"

"I haven't thought about that. I've never been to Niagara Falls, have you?"

"No. I've heard it's beautiful."

"Or maybe we could go to the ocean? I've never been there either."

"That sounds nice too." She smiled. "I'm getting excited."

"*Jah*. Me too. I don't think I'll be able to sleep tonight."

"Neither do I. Okay, then tomorrow it is."

"*Jah*, tomorrow I make you my wife. *Gott* willing." Mahlon smiled.

This was it. This was his answer from *Der Herr*. He bowed his head for a moment and thanked God for His clarity and provision.

TWELVE

Ruth forced her clothes down and zipped up her travel bag. How on earth was she going to sneak out of the house with this undetected? If she got caught, it would ruin everything. *No, I can't take this.*

But she needed clothes. *What am I going to do?* She took the purse she was currently using and changed it out for her larger one, emptying out everything she didn't need. She then rolled up a couple of tops, a skirt, and a pair of capri pants as tightly as she could. Somehow, she was able to stuff them inside. Where would she fit her undergarments? Nothing else was going to be squeezed into her purse, no matter how hard she tried.

Her lunch bag! She hurried to the kitchen, careful not to seem conspicuous, and calmly walked back to her room with it. She took the remainder of her needed items and managed to get them inside.

She was going to be with Mahlon for three days. Her stomach did a little flip-flop at the thought of her and Mahlon getting married and spending the next few days as newlyweds. Was Mahlon as nervous as she was right now?

She looked at her cell phone and realized *it was time*. Time to pretend she was leaving for work, as though she weren't defying her parents and betraying their trust. Time to walk out of the house, as though she would be returning tonight, knowing she would probably never sleep in this home again. Time to remain calm, as though her life wasn't about to change forever.

I can do this.

"Goodbye, Ruthie, have a nice day at work," Mom called.

Her face heated and she suddenly felt like she had a big sign stamped on her forehead that revealed all of her and Mahlon's plans. Did Mom have any idea? Didn't mothers have some type of intuition that told them when their children were doing something they shouldn't?

You're being paranoid. Act natural.

Should she give her mother a hug? Tell her that she loved her, no matter that she was about to turn her world upside down? No, she had to remain inconspicuous, as though it were just like any other day. She couldn't set off any alarms. Even the slightest hint could derail their plans. "Bye, Mom."

As soon as she walked out of the house, she hurried her steps to her car and jumped in. She started the car and began to creep out the driveway.

Until she looked into her rearview mirror and saw her mother waving her arms.

Don't turn around. Just go. She was being paranoid, wasn't she?

But she wasn't about to ignore her mother. If she did, Mom would surely think that something was up. *Play it cool.* She slowly backed up and rolled down her window.

"Did you need something, Mom?" Her hands slightly shook, so she grasped the steering wheel tighter.

Mom handed her a plastic bag. "You almost forgot the sandwich I made for you."

"Oh, silly me." She tittered nervously. "Thanks, Mom. Love you." She quickly placed it on the seat beside her.

"Love you too, Ruthie. Bye."

Ruth rolled the window back up and blew out a breath. She then turned onto the road, ready to leave this place behind. Ready to face her unknown future.

Ready to begin an adventure with the man she loved more than anything.

She couldn't hide the smile on her face if she tried.

THIRTEEN

Ruth took deep breaths as she and Mahlon drove toward the next town east of them. *I can do this,* she told herself.

She spoke into her cell phone. "Hi, Uncle Bill. This is Ruthie. I won't be able to come into work today." She blew out a breath and glanced at Mahlon. "Yeah, I'm fine. I'll see you next week, if that's okay. Thank you. Goodbye."

"Was he okay with it?"

She shrugged. "I hope so."

"You scared?" Mahlon reached over and grasped her hand.

"A little nervous and excited, but not scared. How about you?" She glanced in her rearview mirror to be sure her father hadn't been following them.

"*Jah*, me too, but I think *Der Herr* has given us favor. I prayed yesterday that He would make a way for us to be together. I'm for sure this is His answer." He smiled with confidence.

"You did? You prayed for this?"

He nodded.

"Well, I guess that makes me a little less nervous." She spotted a Walmart sign. "I think we might need rings. Let's buy some at Walmart?"

Mahlon frowned and she could read his disapproval. *Amish don't wear jewelry*, she reminded herself.

"You won't have to wear yours all the time or anything. Just for the ceremony, okay?"

"*Jah*, that's fine, I guess."

Ruth released a sigh, thankful for his concession. If Mahlon was willing to bend on something like this, she had no doubt they could make this marriage work. The thought brought her great comfort, reassuring her they were making the right decision—amid her father's voice of warning echoing in her head.

Nearly an hour later, they stood before the Justice of the Peace. She in a simple white summer dress she'd spotted at Walmart, and he in his *for gut* Amish clothes. Ruth had taken a few moments to change, freshen up her makeup, pin her hair up into a French twist. Mahlon had changed into his Sunday church clothes—a blue shirt, black vest, black pants and matching suspenders, much like he'd worn on their dates.

Ruth had given her cell phone to a stranger and asked if they would snap some pictures for her. Fortunately, Mahlon hadn't objected to the photos, for which Ruth was thankful. He'd been quite agreeable in all of this, although these new concepts must be foreign to him. The more time she spent with Mahlon, the more she fell in love with him, and realized just how blessed she was to have this understanding young man as her soon-to-be husband.

Ruth and Mahlon both kept glancing at the door during the ceremony, half expecting her father to burst through at any moment. Fortunately, he hadn't.

"I, Ruth Johnson, take you, Mahlon Stutzman, to be my lawfully wedded husband…" She completed her vows, staring into her beloved's face while doing so. She couldn't get over how handsome he looked. From this moment on, she'd forever be his.

This was the man she'd be spending the rest of her life with. The man she'd bear children to. The man she'd share all her hopes and dreams with.

After Mahlon repeated his vows, they exchanged the rings they'd purchased at Walmart. Were they actually doing this? Maybe she should pinch herself just to be sure she wasn't dreaming.

"You may now kiss the bride," the Justice of the Peace announced.

Ruth smiled, but she was unsure if Mahlon knew what he was supposed to do. She had no idea how Amish weddings were usually conducted and wasn't sure whether they included a kiss or not. She smiled, leaned forward, and wrapped her hands behind his neck.

Mahlon kissed her appropriately, but it was nothing like their times in the barn. She suspected that he was probably uncomfortable with other people watching them.

They were now married! Husband and wife! Exhilaration filled Ruth as they walked back out to the car, hand-in-hand.

She turned to Mahlon, hardly able to contain her excitement. "We did it!"

Mahlon grinned and pulled her close to him. His lips found hers. "*Jah*, we did, didn't we?" His forehead rested on hers. "Ruthie, my *fraa*."

FOURTEEN

A million thoughts flew through Mahlon's mind as he and Ruthie drove toward their honeymoon destination. He ignored the most worrisome thoughts and determined that he would not address those until he had no choice. Right now, he just wanted to enjoy his time alone with his new wife. *Ach,* he could hardly believe that she belonged to him!

He'd married an *Englisch* girl.

He stared down at the ring on his finger, enjoying the way it felt and the significance it held. Of all the possible outcomes of his life, he never dreamed he'd do something this drastic. No, he thought he'd always toe the line, be the good son, the ever-faithful Amish man. One never knew what the future held, of this thought he was now certain.

He and Ruthie stopped at a restaurant somewhere in West Virginia and ate lunch. While there, she pulled out her cell phone and they determined exactly where they would spend their honeymoon. He was quickly learning how much modern conveniences could come in handy.

"Okay, so we'll find a beach." She smiled and he squeezed her hand across the table.

"*Jah*, that sounds *gut*."

"It says here that there's a boardwalk at Carolina Beach."

"Where's that?"

"It's in North Carolina."

"What's a boardwalk?"

"It's a place where people walk along the beach, usually made of boards. They used to have them lining the main streets in old towns, like the sidewalks we have now. They typically have shops and things for people to do. This one looks like it has an amusement park."

"Really? That sounds like fun. Do they have roller coasters?"

She smiled. "I don't know. Do you like roller coasters?"

"*Jah*. Leon and I went to Hershey Park one time when we were younger. It was a lot of fun."

"Well, I don't know if this will be as exciting as Hershey Park, but it sounds nice."

"It will be exciting if I am with you."

"I most definitely agree. I don't even need an amusement park. We could stay in the motel the whole time, for all I care." She winked and it sent a thrill of excitement through his whole body.

"You don't want to see the ocean?"

"Yes, but with you. I want to enjoy every second we have together."

"Me too, *lieb.*" He took her hand to his lips and kissed it, not caring who was watching.

Mahlon leaned over the seat and nuzzled his wife's neck. "Mm... When are we stopping at our hotel?"

Ruthie laughed. "You're trying to distract me, aren't you? I have to watch the road, honey."

He moved back over to his own seat and picked up Ruthie's cell phone. "Okay, we still have several more hours to go, according to this thing. Are you sure you want to drive all the way through?"

"Well, I haven't made any reservations yet, so we can probably stay just about anywhere. But I'd like to drive as long as possible."

"Okay." He blew out a breath.

Ruthie chuckled. "Are you bored?"

"I'm used to moving—doing things."

"Don't worry. We'll be stopping to eat dinner in just a little bit."

"*Gut*. I can always eat." He smiled.

She reached into the center console and pulled out a small book and pen. "Here. You can do some Sudoku puzzles."

He stared at the book in confusion. "What do I do with it?"

"Okay, see the nine smaller boxes inside the one big box?"

He nodded.

"Each of those nine boxes has nine squares inside. You need to figure out which number goes into each square. It will be a number from one to nine."

"What are these random numbers for that are already written on here?"

"Those are to help you figure out the other numbers. Inside the big box, each row and each column will also have the numbers one through nine." She pointed to a square. "See, the top row for each of these boxes won't have a two, because there is already a two in the third box in this row."

"So, the twos for these two boxes will either be in the second or third row?"

"Right. Exactly. Now look at all the twos on the page. See if you can figure out where the other twos go."

He studied the page. "Ah ha! Here." He placed a two in one of the squares. "And here!"

She briefly moved her eyes to his puzzle book. "That looks right. Now see if you can figure out the rest of the twos, then go on to another number."

"Hey, I like this. This is pretty cool."

"Well, hopefully, it will keep you occupied until we eat."

Ruth yawned. "I'm getting kind of tired. I think we should stop somewhere."

"*Jah*, you've been driving a long time. I wish I could drive some."

"I wouldn't mind, if you had a license."

He reached for her phone. "Let's see. It looks like there's a town coming up. We can probably stop there."

"Which town?"

"Uh, Lexington?"

"Lexington? As in Lexington, Virginia?"

He shrugged. "I guess so."

"Ah, man, too bad it's too late to see anything."

"What did you want to see?"

"I think Stonewall Jackson's house is there."

His brow's shot up. "Who's that?"

She shook a teasing finger at him. "You weren't paying attention in history class, were you?"

"I didn't have a history class."

"You're kidding. The Amish don't teach history?"

"Nope. Well, not like you're thinking. We learned more about Anabaptist history."

"Oh." She shrugged. "Well, Stonewall Jackson was a significant figure in the War Between the States in American history, also known as the Civil War. He served as a Confederate general and commander. He was well-respected and considered one of the best."

"The Amish don't believe in war."

"Well, I guess that's why they wouldn't teach about it then." She pulled the car into the motel's parking lot. "We're here."

Mahlon reached over and caressed her cheek. "Yes, we are."

After checking in, they took the elevator up to the second floor where their room was located. Ruth slid the key into the slot and waited briefly for the green light to appear.

"I enjoy staying in motels. How about you?" She asked over her shoulder as they entered the room.

"*Jah*, especially with my *fraa*." He quickly deposited their bags on one of the chairs. A silly grin accented his handsome face.

Ruth turned back and made sure the locks were in place. "There."

She smiled, allowing her eyes to carefully roam over her husband's face. She took in his height, at least six inches taller than her five-foot-six, then studied his broad shoulders and strong arms—arms she longed to be in.

"Come, *Schatzi*." Mahlon stared for a moment, his gaze examining her as well, then he reached for her hand and brought her near.

She closed her eyes as his lips hungrily met hers, then traveled where they willed. His gentle touch caused her to yield to his every desire, her every desire. The way it should be between a husband and wife.

Who would have thought she'd become a married woman at eighteen? Certainly not her. But, oh, what a wonderful circumstance it was!

FIFTEEN

Ruth glanced out her window as they traveled along the shores of the Outer Banks. "Wow! Look at those houses! They're amazing. Are they built right on the sand?"

"Looks like it. I wouldn't want to live there. It was the foolish man that built his house upon the sand." Mahlon frowned.

"They're so close to the ocean. I think I'd be scared to live in one of them." She could only imagine the destruction if a hurricane ever visited the area.

"*Jah*, I'll keep my farm in Indiana. It *is* really nice here, though. The fresh ocean air feels *wunderbaar*."

"It does. The Outer Banks are a great place to visit, I think."

"For sure, but I'm looking forward to the rides at Carolina Beach."

"I think you'll enjoy Cape Hatteras Lighthouse.

We'll be able to go all the way up to the top."

"*Jah*, I'll like that, for sure."

⁘

"It's too bad they didn't have any roller coasters here. By looking at the photos online, I assumed they did. I didn't know it would just be carnival rides. Sorry I got your hopes up." Ruth frowned.

"It's all right. We still had fun, ain't so?" He came close and nuzzled her neck.

"Oh, yes. We've had lots of fun. I did like the carousel."

"Me too." He grinned.

"I'm kind of sad this is our last day together here. It's gone by so fast." Ruth reclined on the beach chair and let the sand sift through her fingers.

"Kind of? Are you looking forward to going back home?"

"Yes and no. I'm excited to get settled and begin our new life together. They say there's no place like home."

"Except that *you* will have a *new* home." He leaned over and kissed her lips. "With me."

"I'm happy about that, for sure, but I dread facing our parents. I can only imagine what my dad is going to say."

"*Jah*. I 'spect my folks will not be happy either."

"Oh, well. They're just going to have to get used to us being married. I know that *I'm* happy. I don't regret marrying you for one moment and nothing they can say will make me change my mind."

"I'm glad too. So glad. I love you more than anything, Ruthie."

"Anything?"

"Well, except *Gott*."

"Hey, look, Mahlon!" She whispered and pointed. "It's a turtle!"

He looked at her and shook his head. "We have turtles in Indiana too."

"Those are the snapping ones. We don't have these. These are sea turtles."

"They live in the ocean?"

"Yes. They emerge from the ocean to lay their eggs in the sand, then she returns to the water. Then when the babies hatch, they go out to sea too and get carried away by the current. They are nourished and relatively safe within the underwater seaweed forests."

"How do you know so much about them?"

She laughed. "We studied them in school, in my AP science class. We had a small section in our textbook on marine biology. I've always been fascinated by turtles so the teacher captured my attention when he began the lesson on sea turtle migration."

"I never studied science. We didn't have that class in Amish school."

"Really? No science? Wow, that's crazy." She frowned. "But you know a lot about horses."

"*Jah*, for sure."

"So you *did* learn some science. Yours was just more of a hands-on experience."

"I reckon."

She turned back to watch the turtle. "Maybe she's got a nest somewhere around here." Where would the creature stop? "Look, she's building her nest. Did you know that the largest species can get up to two thousand pounds? And they usually have around a hundred babies at a time?"

"A hundred?"

She nodded.

"I think ten would be *gut*."

"Ten turtles?"

"*Nee*, ten *bopplin*. Babies."

She lifted a brow to see if he was joking, but he seemed completely serious. "Really? You'd want to have ten children?"

"As many as *Gott* wills, *jah*. I think ten is a nice number."

"You'd really want *ten* children?"

Mahlon nodded.

She couldn't see herself having that many. Or keeping that many under control, for that matter. In fact, the most children any of her friends' parents had was four. And she'd thought *that* was a large number. It would be something they'd need to discuss in the future.

How many things had they *not* considered before marrying? It didn't matter anyway, she was certain they'd be able to get through whatever challenges life threw at them. She was sure their love would stand the test of time.

SIXTEEN

Mahlon blew out a long breath as Ruthie slowly pulled the car into the driveway of his folks' place. It was time to face the music. What would his parents say? For better or worse, they were about to find out.

"Where should I park the car?"

Mahlon's lips twisted. "How about next to the barn?"

"Okay." She continued up the driveway until the car finally came to the place he'd suggested. She killed the engine and met his gaze. "Are you ready to do this?"

He heard the nervous tone in her voice. It matched his erratic heartbeat. "No, but we'll get through it and it'll be over soon enough, ain't so? *Der Herr* will help us."

She nodded.

He should have been prepared for this. He already

knew *Dat* would be upset when they returned from their honeymoon. But could he ever prepare himself for the disappointment that was certain to accompany his father's gaze? He didn't think so.

They removed their belongings from the trunk and walked to the house. *Dat* met them at the door.

"What is going on here, *sohn*? Where have you and this *Englisch* girl been for the last four days?" His father's voice remained calm but stern. His words were in their native Pennsylvania German language.

"Surprise. Ruthie and I are married now." He chuckled nervously.

Mamm gasped and stood just beyond the screen door, not daring to step out onto the porch. "Mahlon!"

"Married? You…" His father's mouth hung open. He looked from Mahlon to Ruthie and shook his head. There was no way of masking his frown, the look of disappointment that Mahlon hated to see on his father's face. "Why have you done this thing, Mahlon?"

"I love Ruthie. I want to spend the rest of my life with her." He reached for his wife's hand and gently squeezed it. Whether it was to calm himself or reassure Ruthie, he didn't know. His eyes pled with his mother's, hoping she advocate for them.

But his father spoke up. "*Nee*, you are supposed to marry a Plain *maedel*. What have you done? Now, we can never go back home. You have brought disgrace on our family."

"What did you expect me to do, *Dat*? Wait around forever? For *Gott* to drop a Plain girl out of the sky?"

Mahlon grimaced, wishing to shield his new wife from their argument. He hoped that she'd someday learn their language, but now he was glad that she *couldn't* understand their native tongue. His father's words would no doubt sting her as they had him. He could never think of Ruthie—his beautiful wife—as a disgrace. "What's done is done. You may not like it, but whether you and *Mamm* approve or not, she *is* my *fraa* now and your daughter-in-law."

"Then she must become Plain."

"Why? We're not even part of a Plain community. I won't ask her to change. I love her just the way she is."

"Mahlon, your father knows best," his mother's soft voice beckoned beyond the screen door.

"Do not challenge me on this, Mahlon! I am the head of this home. You are not setting a *gut* example for your brother. He will no doubt follow in your footsteps."

"Leon has a mind of his own." Mahlon stood his ground. "And Ruthie is a wonderful *gut* woman. How can she be a bad example?"

"She's an *Englischer*! She is of the world. I can see she has already bewitched you with her ways." His father doffed his hat and furrowed his hair with his fingers. He stared at the ring on Mahlon's finger, as though the sight of it disgusted him. "You will corrupt our ways, Mahlon! And what of any *kinner* you might have? Will you raise them *Englisch*?"

Mahlon frowned. "I don't know. I haven't thought of that."

"It seems as though you haven't thought at all, *sohn*!" His father fumed. "What will you do with her car?"

"Her car? I don't know. We haven't discussed that yet."

"If you keep the car, you will not stay here."

"*Dat*, listen to me. There isn't any other Amish anywhere near us. They won't even *know* that we have a car. If any church leaders ever do show up on our doorstep, they will warn us then. We won't be put in the *Bann* because of it. They will just say that we need to sell it. If that time comes, we can sell the car then. Besides, having a car will be convenient, ain't so? We'll no longer have to pay a driver."

Mahlon's father grunted. "We're not called to live convenient lives, Mahlon. You know that."

"*Jah*, I do. But that doesn't mean that we have to make our lives unnecessarily difficult, does it?" Mahlon did his best to reason, although he wasn't sure he was gaining much ground. "Ruthie is part of our family now. I was hoping you and *Mamm* would welcome her."

His father glanced to Ruthie and lifted a half smile, as though he just realized she'd been standing there the whole time. "*Kumm* in and have some supper. We can discuss this more later."

"*Denki, Dat.*" Mahlon led the way into the house, thankful that his father had conceded—for now, at least. "We're going to put our stuff in my room first." He gestured to Ruthie to follow him up the stairs.

When they reached his bedroom, he closed the door and deposited their bags on the floor. He blew out a long breath.

Ruthie surveyed his simple room.

"It's not much." He hoped she wasn't disappointed.

"It's fine." She smiled. "Are you okay?"

"*Jah.* My father isn't happy, but I didn't really expect him to be." He pulled her close and kissed her. "I love you."

"I love you too." Her lithe fingers moved gently through his hair—something he'd come to enjoy immensely. "I can't wait to sleep in here with you tonight."

His brow shot up. "Really?" He nuzzled her neck.

She nodded. "But right now, we should probably go back downstairs."

"You're right." He smiled. "But I look forward to tonight."

"Me too."

Not long after their return, after the confrontation with Mahlon's parents, and after supper, they were finally able to relax on the porch swing. Ruth smiled down at their intertwined hands as her husband of four days kissed the top her head.

A familiar vehicle pulled into the driveway.

"Oh, no. It's my dad." Ruth took a deep breath and sat up, bracing herself for the conflict that was sure to come.

Ruth's father stormed out of his car and onto the porch. He took firm hold of her arm, hauling her in the direction of his vehicle. "What do you think you're doing going off with Mahlon like that for days? I'm definitely filing—"

"Let my wife go!" Mahlon demanded.

Her father scoffed but stopped in his tracks. "Your wife?"

Ruth held up her left hand. "We're married, Dad. I'm Mahlon's *wife* now and *he* is my *husband*."

"Preposterous! I cannot accept this!"

"It's true."

"What have you done, Ruthie? You've ruined your life!"

"No, Dad. My life is wonderful."

Her father shook his head. "This is ridiculous. You're getting an annulment right now."

"It's too late for that, and I don't want an annulment." Ruth couldn't help the exasperation that clipped her tone. "Dad, Mahlon and I are adults. We aren't children anymore. We *chose* to get married."

He finally released her arm. "What do *his* parents have to say about this?"

"They're not pleased either," Mahlon said, stepping forward, "but they have accepted it."

"Out of all the stupid things to do, Ruthie…and *you*…" He pointed at Mahlon. "You have absolutely no respect for me, or for Ruthie, or her mother. Or for your own parents, for that matter. You had no right to steal *my* daughter and do this thing!"

"Dad, Mahlon and I *love* each other. It's what we *both* wanted. If *you* would have let us date, we would have waited longer to get married, but you gave us no choice!" She brushed away a tear. "And don't blame Mahlon for this. It was my idea."

"I can hardly believe that."

"Dad, we *are* married now. Nothing that you can say or do is going to change that."

"So, what now? Are you going to start wearing dresses and those ridiculous bonnets?" Did her father have any idea how offensive his words sounded?

"It is a head covering, and it's called a prayer *kapp*."

"Whatever."

"How can you accuse Mahlon of not showing respect, when you have insulted their entire Amish culture? Just because they do things differently than you do doesn't mean they're wrong and it certainly doesn't make you any better than them. They're just different." She scowled. "And maybe I *will* start wearing dresses. But if I do, it will be *my* choice. Mahlon has not forced me to do anything, unlike *you*."

He turned to Mahlon. "Do you see what you've done to my daughter? She's *never* spoken to me like this before."

"This is *your* doing, Dad! Mahlon has done *nothing* but love me."

"He has fooled you, Ruthie! He's disregarded my authority and tricked you into marrying him."

"You are not listening to what I'm saying. Nobody tricked me into anything, Dad! We decided this together. This is not just what Mahlon wanted, it's what *I* wanted too. I'm an adult and I have the right to make my own decisions. I shouldn't be forced to go to college when I have no desire to. And I should have the freedom to marry whomever I choose. I chose Mahlon. I love him."

Her father shook his head. "I can see this is pointless. Don't come crying to your mother and me when you've finally realized that you've made the mistake of a lifetime. Goodbye, Ruthie."

Her mouth hung open as she watched her father enter his vehicle then drive down the road. A tear slipped down her cheek unbidden.

Mahlon came up behind her and placed his steady hands on her shoulders. He whispered in her ear. "Shh…it's *allrecht, lieb*."

She turned in his arms and surrendered her emotions, drenching his shirt in the process. Would her relationship with her parents ever be the same?

SEVENTEEN

"I still can't believe that we're married." Ruth reached over her pillow and caressed Mahlon's hair. "Can you?"

He took her face in his hands and brought his lips to hers. "Mm...*jah*, I can believe it."

"I love waking up in your arms, with you by my side. I'm so glad I get to do this every morning. I don't think I'll ever get tired of it."

"Me either." His lips trailed her neckline and shoulder.

"I'm so glad that our parents have finally accepted the fact. I know they still disagree and think we've made the worst decision of our lives, but at least now we won't be badgered by my father or have to worry about him threatening to put you in jail."

"I don't want to talk about our folks right now." He mumbled.

A knock at their bedroom door demanded their attention. Mahlon grunted his disapproval.

"Breakfast, newlyweds," Leon called. "I've already done your chores for a week, Mahlon, and I'm expecting you to pay me back."

"Yeah, yeah. Go on so I can finish kissing my *fraa*." He winked at Ruth.

"You two better come before *Dat* comes and drags you out of bed."

Ruth gasped and whispered, "Would he do that?"

Mahlon shook his head. "Leon's teasing. He's just trying to scare you."

They heard Leon's chuckle through the door, then his footfalls sounded on the staircase.

She rubbed the scruff on his cheek. "When you gonna shave this thing?"

"Shave?" Mahlon frowned. "Don't you like it?"

"It's okay once in a while, I guess." She shrugged. "Beards aren't my favorite thing."

"Married Amish men don't shave their beards, *Schatzi*." She heard his concerned tone.

"Ever?"

He shook his head. "Sorry. I guess I should have warned you." He grimaced.

"If you think *that* would have stopped me from marrying you, you're crazy." She gazed into his gorgeous eyes. "I'll learn to love your beard."

He leaned close and kissed her. "I was hoping you'd say that."

Mahlon abruptly rose from the bed. "Come, *lieb*. Time to start the day. Today, you learn how to be an Amish *fraa*."

"Should I be worried?"

"*Nee*."

"Naomi, will you show me how to make a dress like yours?"

"You want to dress Plain?" Her mother-in-law's eyes widened.

Ruth nodded. "I want to try to do all I can to please Mahlon. If the bishop comes, I don't want him to get into trouble because of me."

"There are many things they could fault him for. Your clothes are only one thing." Naomi smiled. "But Mahlon isn't a baptized member yet, so he wouldn't be put in the *Bann*."

"Do you mean that he won't be shunned? I think I've read about that before or I saw a movie about it."

Naomi laughed. "I hardly doubt that a movie would portray our ways accurately."

"Well, in the movie, they were not able to eat with the family and they couldn't take the shunned person's money."

"*Jah*, those are some things included in the *Bann*. Perhaps I have misjudged." She frowned. "And I fear I have misjudged you too, Ruthie. I will help you make a dress if that is what you would like."

"Thank you."

"And between you and me, I'd say that Mahlon will be pleased with you no matter what you do. They say that love is blind, and I think there is some truth to that. We tend to overlook the faults of our sweethearts, don't we?"

"I think remembering simple things, like doing to others as we'd like them to do to us, will go a long way in a relationship. Don't you think?"

"You are right. If we put others' needs above our own, we can avoid much strife."

"Is that why you and Eli get along so well?"

"*Jah*, and *Der Herr's* blessings." Naomi covered Ruth's hand and briefly squeezed it. "I'm glad that Mahlon chose you. Amish or no, you are a good match for my son."

Tears sprang to Ruth's eyes. "Do you really mean it?"

Naomi nodded.

"Thank you for saying that. It means a lot to me."

❧

Ruth held up her dress and showed it to Mahlon. "Well, what do you think?" She could hardly contain her excitement.

"What is it?"

"A dress, silly. An Amish dress. I made it over the last few days."

His brow dipped. "For you?"

She laughed. "Well, it's certainly not for you."

"You…you will wear that?" The surprise in his expression surpassed what she'd imagined.

She nodded. "I already tried it on. I love it."

"You do?"

"Yes." She frowned. "Aren't you happy?"

"*Jah*, I'm happy, but I didn't expect you to make a dress. You don't have to do this thing for me."

"I know. I want to."

"Will you try it on for me?"

She grinned. "Okay, but you can't laugh."

He frowned. "Why would I laugh?"

"You've never seen me in an Amish dress. I'll probably look funny."

"No, you could never look funny."

"Okay. Turn around so I can put it on."

He crossed his arms over his chest in defiance. "It's a husband's privilege to watch his wife undress."

"Mahlon, turn around. I don't want you to see me until I have it on. I want it to be a surprise."

"But I already know."

She pinned him with a look of warning not to argue with her.

He obeyed with a reluctant huff, but she knew he was smiling.

She quickly changed out of the outfit she was wearing and threw the dress on over her head. It was hard to make sure everything looked okay without a full-size mirror available. She looked down and smoothed out the small wrinkles.

"Okay, you may turn around now."

Mahlon did as told. His eyes roamed her figure, which was probably a little more difficult to make out with the dress on. He began laughing.

Ruth gasped. "You said you wouldn't laugh!"

He shook his head. "I can't help it. You've got it on backwards!"

She looked down at it. "I do?" She smiled.

"*Jah, Schatzi.* Let me help you." He moved close and fingered her neckline. "See this?"

"Yeah."

He moved his fingers to the back of her neck. "This

V that you got back here, it goes in the front."

She laughed. "Oh, is that why it feels like I'm choking myself?"

"Probably." He smiled. "I wouldn't know since I've never worn a dress."

"That's not what I've heard. Your *mamm* said you wore dresses when you were a baby."

He grinned. "*Jah*, I guess I did. But I don't remember."

"I would have loved to see that. I wish your parents had taken pictures of you."

"And *that* is why I am glad we *don't* have pictures." He chuckled.

She pulled her arms inside and turned the dress around. "There, how does that look?"

"Much better." He leaned forward, kissing her nose. "Now, you look like a true Amish *fraa*. Well, except for the hair."

"What's wrong with my hair?"

"Nothing, I like it down. It's just not Amish like that."

"Do you want me to wear it up?"

"I want you to wear it whichever way makes you happy." Mahlon sat on the edge of the bed and removed his socks.

"I love you, you know that?" She moved close and

leaned in to kiss him as his arms wrapped around her waist. "I guess I'll get out of this dress now. Aren't you going to shower?"

He shook his head. "*Nee.*"

"No?" Her brow lowered. "But you need a shower. You've been working in that hot shop all day and you're all sweaty."

He shrugged. "We only bathe once a week. Sometimes twice if something special is happening."

"Once or twice a week? But on our honeymoon—"

"On our honeymoon, we didn't have to worry about emptying out the cistern. *Dat* is worried that we could have a drought here like we had in Pennsylvania. If the cistern empties and we have no rain, we won't have water to use for cooking or laundry."

"Well, you can't come to bed like that, you'll soil the sheets." She tapped her foot, her frustration building by the second.

He shrugged. "I don't know what you want me to say, Ruthie. This is how it has to be."

I don't want our first argument to be about taking a shower. She took a calming breath. *This situation isn't Mahlon's fault,* she reminded herself.

Ruth sighed. "Just a minute."

She quickly went downstairs and fetched a large bowl and filled it with water. She took a bar of soap and a washcloth, and brought them upstairs to their bedroom.

"What are you doing?" Mahlon eyed her with curiosity.

"Take off your shirt." She set the bowl on the nightstand beside the bed.

A sly grin creeped up the side of his mouth. "Hey, I think I like where this is going."

She dipped the washcloth into the bowl of warm water, rubbed a little soap on it, brought it to his chest, and began removing the perspiration and bits of sawdust.

Mahlon reached for her face and pulled her close for a kiss.

She moved back. "Now, I'm not going to be able to do *this* if you're doing *that*. You'll need to cooperate."

He lifted doleful puppy dog eyes and began a mock pout. "Do I have to?"

"Good things come to those who wait."

He smiled. "I'm waiting. Patiently. See how patient I am?"

"Good boy." Ruth laughed. "But tomorrow, you're giving yourself a sponge bath."

His pout returned.

EIGHTEEN

"*Mamm, Mamm! Cumm!*" Leon's voice sounded urgent and Ruth and Naomi both sprang to their feet, tossing their sewing projects aside.

"What? *Was is letz, sohn?*"

"It's *Dat*. Something's wrong!"

Naomi rushed outside, with Ruth close behind her. They followed Leon as he ran to the barn. In a stall, Mahlon knelt next to Eli.

Mahlon's eyes met his mother's. "I think he's had a heart attack."

"I can call 911," Ruth said, ready to race back to the house to retrieve her cell phone.

"*Nee.*" Mahlon put his fingers to his father's neck, feeling for a pulse, as though trying again would make his father come back to life. "He's already gone."

"Gone? No!" The anguish in Naomi's voice caused

each one present to share in her grief. She knelt over her husband's lifeless body and laid her head on his chest. "Eli! You can't leave us. *Gott*, please, no!"

Mahlon stood and pulled Ruth to him, fiercely holding onto her as though his life depended on it. She wept with her beloved as he clung to her, giving what comfort she could.

Leon stooped, rubbing his mother's back, but it seemed to bring little consolation.

Ruth shook inwardly, dreading the day she might have to face such a tragedy. Hopefully, that would never happen. If it did, she'd pray that God would give her the strength to get through it.

Since they hadn't been part of an Amish community, Eli's funeral and burial had been more like an *Englischer's* than an Amish man's.

The days and weeks following had been the most difficult for the family, but mostly for Naomi. Many times, Ruth heard weeping during the night and her heart went out to her mother-in-law. She wished there was something she could do to bring her comfort.

As for Mahlon, Ruth was glad she could console

him. She wished she could give him a child, but it seemed their efforts had been fruitless so far. Maybe someday…

Mahlon stopped hammering when Leon called his name. He'd began working in construction with his brother since their father had passed away. It just made sense—construction brought in more money for the family than his woodworking business.

Ruthie hadn't liked the fact that he'd set aside his dream and now worked away from home, but she understood. She'd even offered to begin working outside the home, which he declined. He wasn't going to let her be the provider—that was his job. He wanted to be her provider. He wanted to be her protector. He wanted to be her everything. Wasn't that what a *gut* Amish man did for his *fraa*?

Leon moved closer. "When you and Ruthie got married, what did you do?"

Mahlon frowned. "What do you mean?"

"I mean, where'd you go? How did you do it?"

"We went to the courthouse and were married by the Justice of the Peace."

"Oh." He scratched his cheek. "Not a preacher?"

Mahlon shook his head and chuckled. "It was short notice and we were kind of in a hurry."

Leon rolled his eyes. "Tell me about it. You should have seen *Mamm* and *Dat*. They were quite upset."

"I can imagine."

"Do you regret it?"

"Not for a second. It's one of the best things I ever did." He rubbed his beard that seemed to be filling out more every day. "Why are you asking?"

"Thinking about something."

Mahlon's brow shot up. "About getting married?"

Leon nodded.

"To that *Englisch* girl you've been courting?"

"*Jah*. Olivia."

"Do you think she's ready? Does she want to become Amish?"

"We've talked about marriage some. I don't think she wants to be Amish, though."

"Mom probably won't be happy."

"I know. But I don't really have a chance of marrying an Amish girl. Besides, I love Olivia."

Mahlon shrugged. "Then marry her, if you think she's a *gut* match."

Leon's grin grew wide. "I think I will. Thanks, Mahlon."

NINETEEN

The moment Mahlon walked through the door, Ruth attacked him with a kiss.

"Whoa, what was that for?" Mahlon chuckled. He removed his hat and placed it on the wall hook just inside the mudroom. He looked around her, most likely to see if anyone else was around to see their public display of affection.

Ruth giggled. "Nothing. Just missed you, is all."

"It smells *gut* in here." They walked into the kitchen.

She gestured to the table, where row after row of filled candle jars cured. "We've been making candles today."

"I see that. Which scents did you make?"

"Vanilla, citrus, and leather."

"Leather?" He chuckled.

"*Jah*, smell it." She removed the lid to one of the jars and handed it to him.

He brought it to his nostrils. "It smells *gut*. Just like a saddle."

"Speaking of saddles…will you teach me to ride Timber?"

"Have you ever ridden a horse before?"

"No."

"I'm not sure Timber is the best horse to learn on, *Schatzi*. He can be pretty feisty at times."

"But you ride him, don't you?"

"*Jah*, sometimes."

"Then maybe I can ride with you."

"I think I'd like having your arms wrapped around my waist." He bent down and kissed her lips, pulling her form near.

"I think I'd like it too." She returned his kiss with vigor.

"Uh…um."

Ruth and Mahlon broke apart at the clearing of Leon's throat. She felt her cheeks growing hot.

"Some of us save that for the bedroom." Leon brought his wife close and winked at her.

"Sorry," Ruth apologized.

She and Olivia moved to clear the table of the candles to prepare for the evening meal.

Mahlon feigned offense. "You're sorry for kissing me?"

She playfully poked his chest. "Never."

"Time for supper, you two lovebirds. You'd think that after a year of marriage, the flame would have died out at least some." Leon grinned.

An entire year and still no fruit from their love. Ruth wanted to give Mahlon a *boppli* so badly, but it hadn't happened. Would they ever be able to conceive? Would Mahlon ever get the children he was so eager to father? A dull ache had formed in her heart—it was the same one that often accompanied her thoughts.

Oblivious to Ruth's musings, Naomi walked in from the kitchen and waved a hand, jumping into the conversation. "Your father and I were married thirty-five years and the flame never died out. As a matter of fact, it grew a little stronger each day." She set five plates on the table.

"Really, Mom?" Mahlon smiled and squeezed Ruth's hand.

"Wow, thirty-five years! It must've been a wildfire." Leon chuckled.

Olivia brought bread and jam and placed it alongside the chow-chow, noodles, and ham they'd prepared for supper.

"For certain sure." Naomi smiled.

"I miss *Dat*," Leon said as he took a seat at the table across from his wife.

"We all do, *sohn*. What I wouldn't give to have him back here." Naomi wiped away a tear.

"I'm sure he don't want to come back to this old place after being in Heaven walkin' on streets of gold," Mahlon said, then they each bowed their head in silent prayer for the meal.

TWENTY

Nine years later…

A knock sounded at the door. "Ruthie, will you get that, please?" Naomi called from the kitchen.

"Sure." She padded to the door and peeked through the window. *A police officer?*

Ruth swallowed and pulled the door open. "May I help you?"

The officer frowned. "Is this the home of Mahlon and Leon Stutzman?"

"*Jah.*"

"Are you related to one of them?"

"Yes, I'm Mahlon's wife. Is something wrong?"

His lips pressed together in a hard line and sympathy darkened his eyes. "Your husband has been in an accident. A vehicle attempted to pass his buggy and didn't see the oncoming car. The buggy was forced off the road and it turned over…I'm sorry, but he didn't make it."

"He didn't make it? Wait. What do you mean? He's... dead?" Her throat tightened so much she could hardly speak.

"I'm afraid so, ma'am."

"No." She shook her head. "No! Not Mahlon!" Ruth sobbed. "He can't be dead!"

Naomi and Olivia surely must've overheard their conversation and appeared at her side.

"And...Leon? Is *he* okay?" Olivia's voice trembled.

"Neither of them made it, ma'am. I'm sorry."

"My sons!" Naomi cried. "Now, I have lost everything. I have nothing."

Ruth ran to her room. She couldn't hear any more. No, Mahlon couldn't be gone! They didn't have enough time together. She didn't even have a little one to remember him by.

She moved to the small closet Mahlon had built in their bedroom and buried her face inside one of her husband's shirts, attempting to capture a remnant of his scent. Tears fell as she realized she'd never sew Mahlon another shirt. Her beloved would never don these clothes again. His strong arms would never be there to wrap around her and hold her tight. His soft lips would never again press against hers. She'd never feel his touch, his caress, his warmth at night.

Oh, Mahlon! Please don't leave me here alone. I

need you. I love you. Ruth couldn't keep the tears from falling. Why did God have to take him so early?

Gone were the dreams of the two of them growing old together. She was now destined to live a life alone. Would she become like her mother-in-law Naomi, who had seemed to age twenty-five years in the time her husband Eli had been gone? Would her eyes hold the same despair, the bitterness of a life of loneliness?

How could she keep on breathing? How could she bear this pain that felt like a hundred bricks pressing down on her heart? Why couldn't *she* have been the one with Mahlon instead of his brother Leon? At least then they would have died together and Olivia would still have her husband.

Her hands trembled as she forced them together and offered an inaudible prayer. *God, please. Take me too. I don't want to keep living if Mahlon isn't here by my side. I don't want to live this life alone. I love him so much, Lord. I'm not ready to let him go. Please! I just can't...*

Ruth hurried down the stairs, through the kitchen, and dashed out of the house. The air inside had become too stifling. The pressure was too much. She couldn't breathe. She sprinted toward the field. Maybe the fresh air would help. Perhaps the sunshine would ease some of this pain.

She crumpled to the ground and hugged her knees,

allowing the tears to fall. This was *so* hard. How could she do this alone? How could she fall asleep each night without Mahlon by her side? How could she live through the toils of this life without her beloved?

"Ten years is not enough, God." Her tears continued to fall as she cried out. "I *need* him here with me."

A nudge on her shoulder caused her to lift her head. *Timber.*

Could he possibly know that his master was gone? She lifted her hand to the stallion's face and rose to meet him. She pressed her face close to the animal, stroking his mane and neck.

"He's gone, Timber. Mahlon's gone. He's not coming back." More tears escaped her lashes.

Timber stood sentry, like a rock of comfort. Did he understand? Was he mourning too?

Somehow, having her beloved's horse there was like having a small piece of Mahlon present. Almost like an embrace from him.

"You understand, don't you, boy?" She rubbed his neck.

She felt the slightest little bit of burden gently lift from her shoulders. Timber knew. He might not fully understand, but he could sense her grief. This usually-spirited animal simply stood with her in her anguish.

Mahlon may have been gone, but he'd left a wonderful gift behind. Timber.

TWENTY-ONE

It had been six months since the death of her husband, yet it seemed like yesterday. Each day Ruth awakened without Mahlon by her side—holding her, kissing her, speaking softly in her ear—the soul-crushing pain returned, reminding her that she was alone, that she'd never again be held by her beloved's strong arms. Would this aching ever stop?

She hadn't been alone in her loneliness, though. She was well aware that Olivia also suffered loss, and she couldn't even imagine Naomi's plight. She now studied her mother-in-law, attempting to fathom what she was thinking. Naomi folded the letter she'd read nearly ten times today, it seemed. Ruth wondered at the contents, but she wouldn't ask. It was none of her business.

"You must go back to your families now, *dochdern*." Naomi's voice sounded resolute, which piqued Ruth's curiosity even more.

Ruth set her sandwich down on the plate and stared at her mother-in-law. "What do you mean? You want us to move out?"

"The drought is long over. The crops are growing well and there's plenty of food now. I'm moving back home to Pennsylvania, to join my people once again. I need to get away from this place and all the heartache it has brought. It's time."

Tears sprang to Ruth's eyes and she shared a bewildered glance with Olivia. "No, I don't want you to leave."

"You and Olivia are still young. You can stay here and remarry *Englischers*. You don't need me here. It's not like I'll have another son for you. There's no sense in wasting your life."

"We will go with you," Olivia insisted.

Ruth nodded in agreement.

Naomi shook her head. "No, it's better if you stay. You can go back to your families, *jah*? There is nothing in Pennsylvania for you."

"She's right, Ruthie. We don't even know anyone there," Olivia reasoned. "At least here we have our friends and family."

Ruth frowned. "But *you* will be there, Naomi. You are all I have left of Mahlon. You have been so kind to me. I won't leave my husband's mother alone. My home isn't with my family anymore, you know how my father felt about Mahlon and me. He never did approve of our union. My place is with you now. You are my family."

"But you have no family in Pennsylvania and mine are Amish."

"Ruthie, Naomi is right. If we stay here, we can remain *Englisch*." Obviously, Olivia had made up her mind to stay. "I'm going to go start packing my things."

Olivia hesitated momentarily and placed a hand on Naomi's forearm. "I will miss you, Naomi. You too, Ruthie. Thank you both for everything. Know that I love you and I wish you the best."

"*Denki, dochder*. I wish you the best as well. *Der Herr* be with you." Naomi turned from Olivia to Ruth. "You should take heed."

Ruth looked after Olivia forlornly as her sister-in-law left to pack her things. How could she give all this up so effortlessly? Did Olivia not feel the same connection she did? This was part of her heritage now, her posterity.

"Being *Englisch* doesn't matter to me. I'll have you. You're the only family I need." Ruth couldn't imagine not taking care of Naomi the rest of her days. That was the Amish way, wasn't it? Since Mahlon was gone, it was her duty now. It was what he would have wanted.

She could at least honor his memory in this way. She couldn't let Naomi go to Pennsylvania all by herself.

"You don't know the ways of my people. You will feel out of place. They might look down on you. You're different from us."

Ruth glanced down at her cape dress. She and Mahlon had sold her car after Eli had passed away, so she was used to traveling in a horse-drawn buggy. She'd already learned many Amish ways. Yes, she'd been born an *Englischer*, she couldn't deny that. But in her heart, she very much felt Amish. "I know I am, but I can learn. You've already taught me so much."

"It's more than just canning and quilting and wearing Plain clothing, Ruthie."

"I know that. I've seen how you and Eli and Mahlon and Leon were. Your devotion. I love your people and your way of life. I want that life for me. For my future. I will go with you." She set her face as a flint. "Where you go, I will go. Your people will be my people. Your God will be my God. I won't leave you."

"Can I not persuade you otherwise?"

"No. I insist on going with you."

"It will be a hard life."

"I'm not afraid. We will have God on our side, right?"

"I don't feel like God's been on my side for many years now."

"That's not true. You have many blessings." Ruth hoped she'd look on the bright side. Life seemed much easier when focusing on everything that was good in life as opposed to focusing on the bad. "You're alive. You're healthy. You still have me."

Naomi seemed to ignore Ruth's words. "I'll contact a realtor tomorrow and we'll leave at the end of the week."

"The end of the week?" It was so soon...

"I plan to sell everything." Naomi's eyes met hers. They'd already sold off most of the farm equipment and animals. She couldn't mean...

Tears sprung to Ruth's eyes. "What about Timber?"

"We'll need to sell him too. We need all the money we can get and it would cost too much to transport a horse. We have no men to support us now."

"But I can work. I don't mind."

"Even so. We will need to sell Timber." Naomi had spoken and there was no sense in trying to change her mind. "I'll call Nelson Harper and ask him to find a buyer or take him to auction."

"Okay." Ruthie reluctantly forfeited her will. She left Naomi alone in the house. She need to flee this place for a while. She needed to be alone. Losing Timber would be like losing a piece of Mahlon all over again.

She walked to the pasture and Timber met her at the fence line. She rubbed his neck like she had nearly every day since Mahlon had gone, as her tears fell. Why did it feel like she was betraying a friend? "I'm sorry, Timber. I'll miss you more than you know."

TWENTY-TWO

Ruth stared out the window of their hired van as the scenery seemed to fly by. She could hardly believe she'd said goodbye to her home state and her former life.

There would be many things that she missed, but it was Mahlon's memory that she cherished the most. And those memories would go with her wherever she went, along with the beloved gift Mahlon had given her so many years ago—her carved horse named after Timber. Yes, Mahlon had given her much in the ten years they'd been together.

"Are you sure I can't persuade you to go back to your family? It's not too late, you know." Naomi squeezed her hand. "You can ride back with the driver."

"Naomi, you *are* my family now. I can't even imagine moving back under my parents' roof. And I already told you that I won't let you take this journey alone. I want you to be in my life. I want to be in your life. You may not realize it, but we need each other."

"Do you plan to become fully Amish then?"

"Yes. That's what I intend to do."

"I don't think you realize what you are asking, *dochder*. It is not as simple as becoming a member of an *Englisch* church."

"I wouldn't know what that's like either."

"We will speak with the bishop then and see what he has to say. He will tell you what is required."

"Well, what did *you* have to do?"

"It will be different for you. You are an *Englischer*. I was born Amish and have been my entire life. I grew up knowing our language and our customs."

"Do you think that I will be required to learn Amish?"

"*Deitsch. Jah*, most likely."

"I tried learning Spanish in school, but I wasn't very good at it." Ruth frowned. "What if I have trouble learning the language?"

"These are questions you'll have to ask the bishop."

"What else will I need to know?"

"You'll probably be required to learn the Articles of Faith. I had to memorize one of the Articles and quote it for the leaders before I could be baptized."

"Where can I find them?"

"It's called the *Dordrecht Confession of Faith.* I have a copy of it that you may read over."

Ruth thought of all the challenges ahead. Life sure would be different in this foreign land, but she was determined to make it work. If not for her own sake, then for Naomi's.

"Look at all that corn! Doesn't it look delicious?" Ruth couldn't quell the enthusiasm in her voice. Pennsylvania had been much more beautiful than she expected.

Naomi gently slapped the reins to urge the pony on. "Much of the corn is already picked. That was only left for the needy. Many farmers leave the rows around their property so those who are less fortunate can go and pick as much as they want."

"Oh, that's so kind of them." Ruth had never heard of this practice before. "So they just let anyone go and pick corn?"

"Or strawberries, or grapes, or whatever they have planted at the time."

"What a blessing to those in need. I can't believe the kindness of some people."

"Well, not everyone does it. It's best to ask to make sure that the farm has this policy. One wouldn't want to steal."

"No, of course, not. Do you think I could go and pick some corn for us?"

"You would want to do that?"

"I'm not afraid of a little hard work. And we'd have plenty to eat." Excitement bubbled in the pit of Ruth's stomach. She could almost taste the corn on the cob.

"I'm so glad you have come with me. I didn't realize it, but you are a blessing to me."

"*You* are a blessing to *me*. You are not only Mahlon's mother, but you've also been a dear friend. How could I not love you? You and Eli raised such a wonderful son and I was blessed to call him my husband." A tear formed at the corner of her eye. "I just wish I could have given you a grandchild."

Ruth thought of the empty ache in her arms and in her heart. Oh, to have a child from her and Mahlon's love. But it wasn't meant to be.

But maybe someday… *Ach,* it was better not to think that way. Mahlon had been blessing enough. It was too much to ask God for another man to love and to possibly bear his children. No, she'd be content just as she was.

After all, at least she wasn't all alone. She had

Naomi and she couldn't ask for a better mother-in-law. She just wished that she could somehow bring a smile to Naomi's face. Her heart ached for Mahlon's mother. Would she ever know joy again?

TWENTY-THREE

Bo King stood on the balcony and noticed a young woman at the edge of his field. Was she a newcomer to the area? How had he missed seeing her before? She appeared Amish in dress, but something about her betrayed her identity. It must've been in the way she carried herself, as though she were an *Englischer.*

He moved down to the main dining area of the house and fetched a snack for himself. Thankfully, his housekeeper had prepared something.

Bo saw one of his workers walk near the front door. "Hey, Mose. Did you see a young woman gathering corn at the edge of the east field?"

"I did."

"Do you know who she is or where she came from?"

"They say she is Naomi Stutzman's daughter-in-law, the widow of Mahlon."

"I see." Bo nodded. He'd been young when his cousin Eli left the area with his family, but he did remember Mahlon. They'd been about ten years apart in age, give or take. "Has she been here many days?"

"Today and yesterday."

Bo frowned. The woman and her mother-in-law must be in need if she was gathering corn in his field. "Mose, I'd like some of the workers to pick a few extra bushels and leave them in piles where she's gathering. Let her know that she's free to take it."

"For sure, Bo."

As Ruth dumped the baskets of corn into the back of the pony cart, a smile spread wide across her face. What good fortune she'd had today! She couldn't wait to get home and tell Naomi all about it.

She hurried the pony down the road as fast as the little guy would trot and tied him up to the hitching post the moment she arrived. She practically ran to the back entrance of the small house she and Naomi were renting.

"Naomi! Naomi!"

"Goodness, *dochder*. What is it?" Her hands were covered in white flour.

"Come see!" Ruth pulled her mother-in-law to the pony cart. "Just look."

"Where did you find all this corn?"

"The farm down the road. I'd been picking most of the day, then I came across several piles just sitting there between the rows. When I enquired about them, the workers said they were free to take."

"How generous. Which farm did you say you were gathering at?"

"It's a couple miles down the road. The large farm with the twin silos."

Naomi nodded with a smile. "That is a cousin of Eli. His name is Bo. He is a kind man to let you take so much."

"I didn't even meet him."

"Well, if he's out there the next time you go, be sure to thank him for his generosity."

"I will, for sure." Ruth smiled. "See how the Lord has blessed us already? I'm certain we made the right decision in coming back here."

"Well, it doesn't look like we're going to starve." Naomi smiled. "We better get that cart emptied out so Cookie can chomp on some grass. It looks like we'll be shucking and canning corn for days."

"It's great, isn't it?" Ruth tempered her excitement.

"*Jah, Der Herr* has granted us favor."

"I enjoy working out there. You know, it seems to help take my mind off losing Mahlon. It's almost like therapy for my soul."

"*Jah*, work can do that, but it doesn't change reality." Naomi's bitter tone stung and threatened to damper some of Ruth's enthusiasm. She refused to dwell on the negative, though. God *had* been good to them.

As Ruth rested her head on her pillow that night, she couldn't get over the farm owner's generosity. A smile played on her lips at the thought of meeting him. Naomi had said that he was Eli's cousin. Was it possible that he was single? If so, maybe he could marry Naomi and they could have a real home again. And just maybe it would lift her mother-in-law's unpleasant disposition. She'd pray for that.

TWENTY-FOUR

Ruth wiped the sweat off her brow as heat caressed her face. The morning sun was hot and it only stood to get hotter. She should go up to the house and get a drink of water. She set down the bushel of corn she'd collected and made her way toward the house.

A man stepped into the row she was walking through and she instantly knew he must be Eli's cousin, whom Naomi had spoken of. Although, he seemed to be a little younger than Eli. Perhaps in his mid-forties?

"Hello, sister. I'd like to introduce myself. I am Bo King, and these are my fields." Kindness lit his eyes.

She smiled. "I am Ruth Stutzman. My friends call me Ruthie. I am Naomi's daughter-in-law. I want to thank you for allowing me to glean in your fields. Naomi and I really appreciate it."

"It's nice to meet you, Ruthie. I'd be pleased if

you'd do all your gleaning here. There's no need for you to go into others' fields. I have plenty and a good variety. You and Naomi are welcome to take all that you need." He gestured toward the house. "And if there's anything else you're in need of, please come to the house and let me know. Make sure you drink plenty out in this heat and be sure to rest once in a while. I would not want you to get dehydrated."

"Thank you. Your kindness means a lot."

"I've asked the young men not to bother you. You will be safe here. You can work alongside my female workers if you wish."

"*Denki*. I…" She felt like crying. The Lord had been so good to her. "This is a wonderful blessing, Bo King."

"You may call me Bo." He nodded. "God has blessed me greatly. I cannot help but share those blessings." He pointed toward the fields. "I was on my way to check on the work my employees have done."

"I was going to get a drink of water."

"Then don't let me keep you. Have a *gut* day, Ruthie." He tipped his hat and continued walking in the direction he'd been headed.

Ruth felt like she could give this man a hug. But that wouldn't be appropriate. She learned some things since becoming Amish and had found that public displays of affection were frowned upon. Mahlon was a bit more affectionate than most Plain folk, but even he had been subdued in the presence of others.

She turned and stared after Bo until he walked out of sight. What kind of man was he? She didn't think she'd ever met anyone quite like him. His eyes held a depth to them that one could get lost in. He seemed content, yet she sensed a subtle sadness somehow. How many layers did he possess underneath his handsome exterior?

Handsome?

Yes, she supposed he was, in a rugged sort of way, for a man of his age and experience. The gentle greying of hair near his ears reminded her of a popular actor she'd seen on TV many years ago. His beard only showed minimal signs of age but somehow it enhanced his attractiveness. But even considering all those positive outward qualities, the most attractive thing to her was him.

Bo. The man. His soul.

It seemed as though he could be an easy best friend—a trusted friend. His tone was so gentle and soothing, like he could put one's mind at ease just by conversing with them.

She blinked, realizing she'd been standing there daydreaming for far too long. She chided herself for being so foolish and hurried to fetch her drink of water before eventide rolled in.

What on earth had possessed her to be thinking on another man like that? No one could ever replace Mahlon. No one.

"I met Bo today and thanked him." Ruth looked over her supper plate at Naomi.

"He's a generous man, *ain't so*?"

Yes, that was one word to describe him. What other qualities did this man possess? "Do you know much about him?"

"Not really, just that he has a very good reputation. Whenever Eli had mentioned him in the past, he always spoke highly of him."

"He seemed very kind."

"That, he is."

TWENTY-FIVE

Ruth looked to the west where the sun was rapidly making its descent. It was about time to begin heading in the direction of home.

"Ruthie, Bo said there is an extra box of fruit for you up at the house. He said to be sure to stop by and get it before you leave."

"*Denki*, Mose." She watched as Bo's employee walked off.

Ruth finished up the task at hand and set off toward the main house. She spotted Bo as she stepped onto the porch.

"I see you've found your way. Your box is in the basement, where it is cool. I will get it for you." She couldn't deny Bo's attractive smile. He seemed to have some type of inner joy that touched everything he said and did.

Ruth's heart filled with gratitude. "Why are you

being so kind to me? I don't deserve any of this."

"Ruthie, I only give because of what's been given to me. Because of that gift, my heart overflows." His eyes pierced hers, as though he could see into her soul. "Have *you* met the Saviour?"

"The Saviour?"

Bo smiled. "Jesus Christ, the gift giver."

She shook her head.

"Would you like to?"

"I…don't know. I think so." She nodded. "But how can I? Isn't Jesus dead?"

He chuckled. "Oh, no. He is very much alive! He speaks to me every day. And I talk to Him every day."

She frowned. Maybe this was why he wasn't married. Was he delusional? No, there had been no other outward indication of that. He'd only been kind.

She'd give him the benefit of the doubt. "But how? I don't understand."

"Come with me." He held out his hand. She took it and let him lead her into his house. His easy demeanor set her mind at ease and she knew she had nothing to fear.

She looked around to see if anyone was nearby. Was this proper behavior for an Amish woman? She didn't want to do anything wrong or anything that might cast doubt on Bo's character. But he didn't seem to be worried at all.

"Come, sit here." He gestured to the small table in the breakfast nook.

She looked out the windows of the octagonal room. "You have a great view here. Your place is very nice."

He nodded and joined her at the table, Bible in hand. "God has been very gracious to me."

"Who lives here, besides you?"

"It's just me."

"Have you...? I know it's really not my place to ask..." She let her words trail off.

"You may ask whatever you'd like. I have nothing to hide."

"Have you ever been married?"

His gaze sobered and he stared out one of the windows. The hint of sadness she'd detected earlier returned to his eyes. "When I built this place, I dreamed of one day filling it with children—with a family of my own." He frowned. "But the Lord has never seen fit to bless me with a wife."

Ruth mulled over that thought in her mind. There was no reason, that she could see, why Bo shouldn't be married. He was kind, handsome, generous, wealthy, and who knows how many other great qualities he possessed that she knew nothing about. A man of his caliber would no doubt have a laundry list of wonderful traits. She'd never heard anyone speak ill of him, not that she'd been here all that long. The thought baffled her.

"I…lost my husband." She shared.

Bo nodded. "Mahlon, Eli's son." His hand briefly covered hers and he gently squeezed. "I know. I'm sorry for your loss." His eyes conveyed understanding, compassion.

In that moment, she felt like she could share anything with this man. He could be trusted. She could share her deepest hopes, her darkest secrets, her most daring dreams, and he would understand.

"*Denki.*"

TWENTY-SIX

Bo thought about what he'd said to Ruthie. He'd wanted to tell her that his mother had been an *Englischer* too, just as she. But he didn't wish to tell her all that was on his mind—that his bachelorhood was most likely due to the fact that his mother had been *Englisch*. Because everyone knew that jumping the fence was the worst thing that could happen to an Amish person. He may have been well-respected, but he often wondered if those in the community *truly* trusted him.

He gestured for her to take the seat across the table from him and she did as told.

He opened the Bible in front of him and turned to a passage and read. *"The Spirit of the Lord is upon me, because he hath anointed me to preach the gospel to the poor; he hath sent me to heal the brokenhearted, to preach deliverance to the captives, and recovering of sight to the blind, to set at liberty them that are bruised.*

"Ruthie, do you believe the words of Jesus? That he was sent to heal the brokenhearted?"

She shrugged. "I'm not sure. I don't know much about the Bible."

"The Bible is God's love letter to mankind. Israel were God's chosen people. He loved them and pursued them, but they kept turning away from Him.

"God had said to Israel that He would turn their mourning into joy, that He would comfort them and make them rejoice in their sorrow. But they needed to turn to Him, to depend on Him for their every need. I believe He wants to do that for you too, but you'll need to trust Him with all your heart."

"I'm not sure if I know or understand how to do that," she said.

Bo loved and appreciated Ruthie's honesty.

"Ruthie, I can tell by what I've seen and heard of you so far that you have a pure heart, that you care for others, that you put others' needs above your own. And I find that admirable. But even the kindest person still has a huge obstacle to overcome when it comes to a relationship with God. And that obstacle is sin."

"Sin?"

"That's right. It's our sin that separates us from God. When Jesus died on the cross and shed His blood, He did it so our sins could be washed away. On the third day, He arose from the grave, proving that He had indeed conquered sin and death and hell."

She frowned. "Why?"

"Well, when God made man, His plan was to have a relationship that lasted forever. When man sinned, he erected a wall of separation between mankind and God. And that sin was what brought death into the world. Before sin, there was no death, no pain, no suffering. The only way to purge that sin was through the shedding of blood. But for sin to be pardoned forever, the sacrifice had to be perfect in every way.

"That sacrifice was Jesus. He *chose* to come down to earth and give His life for you and me. He knew, that if He did this, it would be a grave sacrifice on His part. Can you imagine coming down from Heaven—a place of total peace and joy and happiness, where there is no pain or sorrow or death—to this crazy world where people are filled with hate and are killing each other? And *knowing* all of that and that *you* would be tortured and killed after you've lived a completely sinless, selfless life… It hurts my heart to even think of the anguish He must've gone through for my sake."

"Wow. I…I never realized that that's who Jesus was and why He died on the cross. I mean, I'd heard of it, but the way you just explained it—it makes more sense now. I still don't fully understand *why*, though."

"That part is simple. He loves us and He wanted to make a way for us to live forever with Him in Heaven. It is not His will that *any* go to hell. The way to Heaven is free. All we have to do for our part is believe."

"Just believe?"

"Here's one of the most beautiful passages in the Bible. Listen closely.

"For God so loved the world, that he gave his only begotten Son, that whosoever believeth in him should not perish, but have everlasting life.

"For God sent not his Son into the world to condemn the world; but that the world through him might be saved.

"He that believeth on him is not condemned: but he that believeth not is condemned already, because he hath not believed in the name of the only begotten Son of God."

"So those who *don't* believe are condemned? Does that mean they go to hell?"

"As far as I understand it. But God is not unrighteous in this." Bo shook his head. "God made a way for *every* man, woman, and child to be saved. And that way cost Him His precious Son. Can you imagine offering your own child and seeing what that child endured, only for people to reject your gift? I know, I can't. God made salvation so simple, one would be foolish to reject what He's offered freely."

"I would like to receive His gift, to accept His offer. What do I need to do? Do I pray?"

"You may, if you'd like. God already sees your heart. He reads your thoughts. He knows everything about you. Just talk to Him as if He's standing right here in our midst, because in actuality, He is."

She looked around. "He is?"

He smiled. "You cannot see Him. The Bible says that when two or three are gathered in His name, that He is in their midst."

Ruth had never heard these things all her life. Could what Bo was saying actually be true?

"Okay, wow. Then I guess I'll..." She bowed her head and took a deep cleansing breath. "God..."

Her tears began to flow and she couldn't speak for several seconds. "Thank you *so much* for what You've done, for what Jesus did for me. I can't even imagine... Please, I want to have everlasting life with You. I want this joy that Bo has. I believe in what You've done. I want Your gift. Thank you, Lord."

She looked up and again saw *something* in Bo's eyes. Goodness, perhaps?

"Thank you so much for sharing that with me."

He smiled. "There's nothing more pleasurable than sharing God's love with another human being. I'll never tire of it."

A clock alerted them to the time.

"I'd better go. Naomi will wonder where I've been. I don't want her to worry."

"Did you drive today? If not, I could give you a ride."

"I brought the pony cart, but thank you for offering, Bo." She didn't think she'd ever met a more considerate man.

"Will I see you at meeting on Sunday, then?"

"I should be there. I'm a little nervous, though. It'll be my first time."

"Ever?"

She nodded.

"Has Naomi prepared you at all? Do you know what to expect?"

"Not really."

"How much do you know about it?"

"Not much. Just that it will probably be in a different language and I won't understand."

"Did she tell you how long it lasts?"

"No."

"It's about three hours or so, depending on whether

they have business to discuss or not or if it's a special meeting."

"Three hours?" Her eyes bulged.

He chuckled. "*Jah*, I realize that it's not the Amish way to just sit around and do nothing. But it *is* the day of rest. And there is always the common meal afterwards."

"She did tell me about that. I'm glad she'll be there with me to guide me."

"I'm sure she will." Bo smiled. "Did she tell you that the men and women sit on opposite sides of the room?"

"She may have mentioned that."

"And the singing is quite different to folks who have never experienced an Amish meeting."

"Like how?"

"Well, you've heard songs on the radio, right?"

"Thousands."

"They're nothing like that."

"Will you sing one for me?"

He chuckled. "I don't think I'm that brave. Besides, it would take about twenty or thirty minutes."

"For *one* song?"

He nodded.

"No wonder the church service lasts three hours!"

"The songs are in German and there are no notes to follow along with in the *Ausbund*. The tunes have been handed down for generations, so don't be surprised if folks sing a little off-key." His laugh was easy.

"The *Ausbund*?"

"The Amish hymn book."

"Yikes. So, the whole thing will be pretty foreign to me, I'm guessing."

"Probably. But you'll survive."

"Would it be frowned upon if I brought a notebook and pen and took notes?"

He grimaced.

"I'll take that as a yes. So, I'll just bring my Bible then?"

He shook his head.

"No Bible, either?" Her eyes widened. "Is there anything *else* I should know before I make a fool out of myself?"

"Try not to fall asleep." He chuckled.

"Have *you* ever?"

"I don't think so, but there are some that do every service."

"Really?"

The clock chimed again.

"*Ach*, you'd better go, Ruthie. Let me get that box of fruit for you and I'll carry it out to your pony cart."

"Thank you, Bo."

TWENTY-SEVEN

"I'm nervous about attending the church meeting." Ruth fastened the apron on her dress just before stepping out the door, remembering the first time she'd tried her Amish dress on for Mahlon. They'd sure gotten a laugh out of that. Oh, how she missed him. She'd always thought her first time visiting an Amish church would be with him.

Naomi placed their contribution for the common meal into the pony cart. Ruth was careful not to step on the box of canned corn between them on the floorboard.

"Nothing to be nervous about," Naomi assured, taking the reins in her hands.

"I am a little more at ease since talking to Bo, though."

Naomi's brow quirked up. "You've been talking to Bo?"

"Yes. He's a very kind man."

"*Jah*, he is. It's a shame he never married. Certainly a good catch for any *maedel*." She kissed the air to propel the pony cart forward.

"Why do you suppose he never married?"

"Could be that his mother was *Englisch.*"

"*What?* I had no idea! But she converted to the Amish way?"

"*Jah.*"

A burst of excitement filled Ruth as she thought of Bo's mother. Yet another thing they had in common. If Bo's mother could convert from *Englisch* to Amish, surely she could too.

Just as Bo had said, the meeting had been lengthy. Glad to finally be off the hard wooden benches, Ruth now took a pitcher around to tables the men had set up, filling the men's and older women's drinking glasses with water. She carried a carafe of coffee in the other hand to serve their pleasure.

"*Denki.*"

Ruth glanced down at the possessor of the familiar masculine voice. She smiled. "Hi, Bo."

"What did you think of the meeting?" A teasing smile graced his lips as though he could read her thoughts.

"It was…interesting." She turned at the sound of Naomi's voice calling. "I'd better go."

She quickly attended Naomi's side.

"You shouldn't be talking with Bo like that," Naomi whispered.

"What do you mean?"

"People will talk."

Ruth frowned. "About?"

"We don't want to get any rumors started. It is already well known that you've been gleaning in his field, and others have mentioned you going up to the house."

"But I—"

"We'll discuss this later—at home." Ruth didn't miss Naomi's abrupt tone and pointed look, indicating the discussion was over for now.

"Okay." Ruth nodded. She'd have to stay away from Bo if she wasn't supposed to be talking to him. Who would have thought that just lingering an extra moment out of common courtesy would get tongues wagging?

TWENTY-EIGHT

A smile played on Bo's lips as he spotted Ruthie in his field. She hadn't been out there every day, but he suspected that was because she'd been busy at home helping Naomi. He didn't doubt they spent hours canning the harvest like his mother used to.

She lifted a hand when she spotted him heading her way.

"It wonders me why you haven't gone with the young folks. You are still at the age where you could find a husband if you were looking for one."

She shrugged. "I'm content as I am. God already blessed me with a good husband and a good marriage. Even though I lost Mahlon, I'm still quite fortunate."

He nodded. "Do you think God would only have you marry once?"

"I don't know. If it *is* His will that I remarry, I pray that He will make it clear to me. I wouldn't want to enter a marriage of my own accord. You know what I mean?"

"*Jah*, I do. You want to follow God's plan for your life. That's admirable, Ruthie. That is what I've always wanted too."

"But God has never prompted you to marry?"

He shook his head. "I've never felt God leading me in that direction."

"When did you get baptized, if you don't mind me asking?"

"I was eighteen."

"Did you have a difficult time of it?"

He frowned. "Difficult? What do you mean?"

"You know, learning the *Articles of Confession* and all that."

"It wasn't too bad."

"Well, *I* am having a time of it. Not to mention, Naomi is trying to teach me Pennsylvania German. At this rate, I don't know if I'll ever be ready to join."

His eyes widened. "You're going to be baptized and become Amish?"

"I'm trying." She blew out a breath. "It's a lot harder than I thought it would be."

"A little more difficult than becoming a child of God, right?" He smiled. "I could help, if you'd like."

"Really?"

"I taught school for a few years when they didn't have any qualified *maed* to do it. I really enjoyed it and I *think* the scholars liked me." He chuckled.

"I think I can picture you as a teacher." She smiled. "That would be great. But when would we find time?"

"You could stay an extra hour later every day or come an hour early. We'd study out on the porch for propriety's sake, of course."

"Where have you been?" Naomi's voice seemed fraught with worry.

"Oh, I'm sorry. I forgot to tell you yesterday. Bo offered to help me with studying for the baptismal classes."

Her eyes widened. "He did?"

"Yes." Ruth smiled.

After a moment of hesitant silence, Naomi took Ruth's hands in hers. Ruth sensed her mother-in-law had something important to say. She couldn't read the look in her eye, but knew she was intent on *something*.

"Do you like Bo?" Naomi asked.

"*Jah*, very much so. He's been a wonderful friend." She hesitated. "Why do you ask?"

"I don't know why I didn't see this before. I should have noticed."

"Noticed what?"

"You and Bo. You are the one he's been waiting for all these years. Don't you see, Ruthie? It's perfect. If Bo will marry you, we will have a place to live. We'll have a man to care for us again. I won't have to worry about your provision, should I pass on. And if the Lord wills, He will give you children."

Ruth held up her hands. "Wait. You want Bo and me to *get married*? He's like fifteen years older than I am. Wouldn't that be frowned upon?"

"So you're *not* opposed to the idea?"

"I...I don't know. I guess I didn't really think..."

"You like him, don't you?"

Ruth nodded.

"And it's plain to see that he's taken with you. You two are a *gut* match, Ruthie."

She wasn't going to argue. She did care for Bo. And as absurd as Naomi's suggestion was, it wasn't an impossible proposition.

"I'm...I just don't know what to say."

Naomi beamed. "Let's bake a pie. You can take it over to him tonight and the two of you can talk about marriage."

"But—"

"There's no 'buts.' Trust me, Ruthie. He will be thrilled with this idea." She waved a hand in front of her face. "And don't worry about your age difference. Many have gotten hitched with much more years in between. Besides, people will just say that Bo got lucky finding himself a younger *fraa*."

Ruth sucked in a breath. "Oh, boy."

TWENTY-NINE

Bo stepped out onto the porch to gaze up at the stars. The heavenly lights twinkled as they had each night, but the air seemed as though it took on a mesmeric aura of anticipation, of joy. He couldn't put his finger on it exactly, but this night felt different somehow.

This night, like others, was beautiful indeed. The air was warm, yet held a crispness to it. Maybe he would sleep out on the porch tonight in his hammock. How long had it been since he'd done that?

He quickly fetched a blanket, then snuggled into his hammock. Falling asleep might be difficult since he felt so energized, but after several minutes he felt himself yielding to dreams in the night.

Were those footsteps he heard? He startled awake and rubbed the drowsiness from his eyes. They widened when he spotted Ruthie walking up the porch steps. Was he dreaming?

"Ruthie?" He sat up.

"I'm sorry it's so late." She seemed timid.

"Why are you here?" He glanced at her hands and noticed she was carrying something. "Is that a pie?"

She smiled. "*Jah*. From the fruit you gave us."

She must've had something on her mind. Why else would she come here at this late hour? He hoped nothing was wrong.

He stood from the hammock. "Let me make some coffee and we can enjoy it with that pie."

A few moments later, they sat out on the porch with coffee and pie in hand.

"Do you want to tell me why you came all the way over here tonight?" He raised a brow.

"I…hope you don't mind."

"No, not at all. I'm just…a little curious."

She blew out a breath then twisted her *kapp* string between her fingers. *Was she nervous?* "This might sound strange and I'll totally understand if you reject this idea…"

"Please, speak what's on your heart."

"When I returned home this evening, Naomi suggested something. At first, I thought the idea was crazy, you know? But the more I thought about it…" She swallowed. "Well, what do you think about us? About marrying me?"

He felt like his eyes might jump out of his head. Did she just say what he thought she said? *Jah*, he *must* be dreaming. He set his coffee down on the small table between them, lest it slip from his fingers. "You...*you'd* consider marrying *me*?"

"I know it seems sudden but—"

"Yes! A thousand times, yes." If he'd ever felt a prompting—no, a downright confirmation—from the Lord, this was it. Hadn't his soul been leading this direction since the day he'd met her? He'd felt this overwhelming urge to care for her, to protect her. She was kind and beautiful and beyond *any* dream he could conjure up.

"Naomi thought that we would make a good match and she's worried about my provision after she passes on."

He frowned. "Is she sick?"

"No, not that I know of."

He took her hands in his and looked into her eyes, searching their depths for absolute truth. "Ruthie, is this what *you* want?" The question was difficult to ask, because it gave her a chance to reject him outright. But he didn't want her against her will.

"Yes."

"You're sure and certain?"

A shy smile graced her face and her eyes met his. She nodded.

He shook his head. "What good fortune! I don't know what you see in a man like me—"

"A man like you? There is none better, Bo. Truly. I am honored that you have agreed to this."

He reached out and caressed her cheek. He could kiss her right now, but he wouldn't. Not until she officially belonged to him. *Wow.*

"I'll need to go and speak with the bishop first thing tomorrow. He…may not approve." He grimaced.

Ruthie frowned.

"But don't worry." He rubbed her hand. "*Derr Herr's* will shall be done."

She nodded.

"Stay here tonight. It's too late to go back home. We'll stay out here on the porch, then I'll walk you home in the morning before the town awakens."

"Thank you, Bo."

THIRTY

Ruth's eyes flitted open as the sun's rays caressed her eyelids. How long had she slept? The last thing she remembered was saying goodbye to Bo. Neither of them had slept at all the prior evening. They'd talked into the early morning hours, as though they'd been good friends their entire life. He'd dropped her off before the townsfolk began to stir, so as not to get tongues wagging. She suspected *he* hadn't gotten any sleep.

Bo. Her soon-to-be betrothed, if the Lord willed.

A mixture of giddiness and sheer anxiety filled her heart. What would the bishop say when Bo went and spoke with him today? What if he declined their request?

"So, how did things go last night?" Naomi's voice aroused her from her thoughts.

Ruth smiled. "Better than I expected. He's going to talk to the bishop today."

Naomi reached for her hand. "This is *Gott's* will for you. I am sure of it."

"I hope you're right." She chewed a fingernail. "Naomi, how do you think Mahlon would feel? You know, about me and Bo."

She expressed a gentle sad smile. "He would want this for you, *dochder*. For certain, he'd want you to be happy."

Bo still had a difficult time convincing himself that last night hadn't been just a dream. Yet, Ruthie had still been there in the morning until he'd taken her home. And here he was now, pulling his buggy onto the bishop's property.

The bishop ushered Bo into his home. The deacon and minister were present as well, as he'd requested.

"What is this matter you wish to discuss with us?"

"I'll get straight to the point. I'd like to marry Naomi's daughter-in-law, Ruthie."

"The *Englischer*?" The deacon rubbed his beard and eyed the other two leaders.

Bo nodded. "She's taking membership classes to join the church."

"And you wish to marry her after this, I presume?" The bishop said.

"*Jah*. As soon as possible."

The men chuckled.

"Is there not someone who might be better suited to her? Jerome Borntreger, perhaps?" The minister suggested.

Bo gritted his teeth. The widower was indeed a better match for Ruthie. He was ten years younger than Bo and he had three children who needed a mother. Children that Ruthie, no doubt, would long for. But she hadn't asked Jerome. She'd come to *him*.

He suppressed the jealousy that threatened to emerge.

"I can speak with him first, if you'd like." He wouldn't mention that Ruthie didn't even know this man. She'd have the final say so.

"*Jah*, that would be best." The bishop confirmed. "If he declines, you are free to marry her after she has completed her classes.

Lord, please let Jerome not be interested in marrying Ruthie. He knew it was a long shot, but he prayed just the same. Hadn't he already felt confirmation from God that he and Ruthie were meant to be together? Or was that just his own anticipation and overzealousness? He couldn't be sure, as doubts now flooded his mind.

Fear reached inside and grabbed a hold of his heart

as he dismounted his buggy and marched toward Jerome Borntreger's barn.

"Bo? What brings you out here today?"

He'd conceal his interest in Ruthie the best he could.

"*Hallo*, Jerome." He shook his hand. "There's this matter, you see. Naomi's widowed daughter-in-law is looking to get hitched. She does have a small piece of land that belonged to her husband's family that whoever she marries would inherit."

"I'll marry her," he said matter-of-factly. "My *kinner* need a *mamm*, and I could do with a good woman around."

Bo's heart plunged. *God, no. Please…*

"Wait a minute. Isn't that the *Englischer*?" His brows knit together in the middle.

"Yes." He wouldn't volunteer any unnecessary information. He wouldn't list her myriad of great qualities. He wouldn't give Jerome one more reason to say yes.

"*Nee*, I don't think I will. Now that I think about it." He waved a hand in front of his face. "Too much drama to deal with. And then, who knows how she might could sway the *kinner* toward *Englisch* ways."

"Are you declining?"

"*Jah, for sure*." He nodded and scratched his beard. "Say, why don't *you* marry her? You ain't never been hitched."

Bo cocked his head to the side, as though he were thinking on the idea. "You know what? I think I might just do that."

He patted Jerome's back. "Thanks for the advice, brother."

"Anytime."

Bo smiled to himself as he drove back down the road. He blew out a relieved breath and hollered louder than necessary. "Thank You, Lord!"

Now, to share the news with Ruthie.

Ruth attempted to keep her mind on her sewing project, but she just couldn't focus right now. Where was Bo? Was he still conversing with the bishop? What was the bishop's verdict?

She finally set her quilt squares to the side and stood up.

Naomi chuckled. "He'll be back soon."

"I know. I'm just…anxious."

"I think I hear buggy wheels."

Ruth practically ran to the window. "He's smiling!"

"Calm down, *dochder*."

She threw the door open as soon as she saw him heading toward the house.

"Good afternoon." Bo grinned as he approached the house. He and Ruth shared glances.

"Would you like to come in for a snack?" Naomi suggested.

"That would be great." He stepped inside and removed his hat.

Ruth could stand the anticipation no longer. "Well?"

Bo chuckled, then he reached for her hands. He gazed into her eyes. "They said yes."

Ruth felt like she could sprint outside and do a thousand jumping jacks and run ten miles. But she'd rather stay here with Bo.

"After you've completed your classes and joined the church, we're free to be published." He smiled. "Do you think you'll be ready by fall?"

Ruth blew out a breath. "I don't know. I hope so. I still have a lot to learn."

"Well, it looks like you and I will be spending a lot of time together." He winked.

She felt her cheeks warm at his affectionate gesture. "I'm looking forward to it."

"Me too."

"Okay, let's go over the *Dordrecht Confession of Faith* again," Bo instructed.

"I'm so glad that I don't have to memorize these. Naomi had me scared." She blew out a breath and leaned back in her chair.

"Articles One and Two?"

She stared out past the porch and tried not to let herself get distracted by the activity in the fields. "Okay, let's see. One—'God and the Creation of All Things.' Two—'The Fall of Man.'"

"Very good. Which Articles did the class review this week?"

"We're on Eleven and Twelve – Foot Washing, and The State of Holy Matrimony."

"Holy Matrimony?" Bo's brow quirked and a gentle smile formed on his lips. "That means you only have two more classes before Baptismal Sunday, right?"

"Yep. Just six weeks!"

"Are you confident?"

"I think so. You know, when I began my classes, I was just doing it to join the church. But now, I feel more excited about finishing so I can marry you. Is that wrong?"

His grin widened. "I don't think so. You just have a little extra incentive."

"I feel kind of out of place being the only older

person in the group. I think everyone else is under twenty."

"That doesn't matter. You were never Amish, so it's going to be different for you." He reached over the table between them and rubbed her hand. "I asked if we could be first in the lineup for our wedding."

"And they okayed it?"

"I think they may have pushed someone else back to accommodate us." He smiled and winked. "There are advantages to being older. They probably figured I've waited long enough." He chuckled.

"You just had to wait until God brought along the right one."

"Indeed."

THIRTY-ONE

"I'd like to invite Olivia to the wedding. Do you think she'll come?" Ruth slipped the invitation she'd just written into an envelope.

"That's a *wunderbaar* idea, I think." Naomi nodded. "How about your folks?"

She frowned, thinking of her family. "I...don't know. They never were too fond of my and Mahlon's relationship."

"*Ach*, you and Mahlon were young when you got hitched. I think they should be over that by now." She dismissed the words with her hand. "You don't think they would be happy to know that you've found a *gut* man to marry?"

Ruth shrugged. "I guess it wouldn't hurt to send them an invitation."

"*Nee*, it wouldn't. And leave the rest up to *Gott*." Naomi's needle plunged into the quilt top she'd been working on. Although she hadn't mentioned anything, Ruth guessed it was to be a wedding gift for her and Bo. It seemed Naomi had been a bit more vigorous since plotting Ruth and Bo's nuptials. Ruth smiled as a soft hum lifted from Naomi's lips.

This marriage would be a surely good thing for all of them, she suspected.

Today was a bittersweet day for Ruth. She'd alternated between tears of joy and tears of sadness all last night. Marrying a wonderful man like Bo would surely be a blessing, no doubt. But somehow she felt like she was letting go of a piece of her heart, letting go of their hopes and dreams, letting go of Mahlon—something she never intended to do.

She slipped into the new blue dress she'd sewn for the occasion and pinned on her white apron. This was certainly different from the way she and Mahlon had gone about their wedding. She remembered the simple white summer dress she'd spontaneously purchased at Walmart just before their impromptu wedding. She'd never worn it again. Those were crazy days, but, oh, how happy they'd been in their blessed ignorance of the trials to come.

She sighed and managed a cleansing breath. *This is the day which the Lord hath made, I will rejoice and be glad in it.*

Dear God, please help me to enjoy this day and to think of my soon-to-be husband, Bo. He is such a good man and I thank You for him, Lord. Help me to be a good wife and helpmeet to him. Remind us to keep You at the center of our lives and our relationship. Thank You. Amen.

What was Bo thinking right now? Was he apprehensive at all? Did he have any doubts? After all, she'd been the one to approach him about marriage. Was he simply performing out of duty or did he really love her? Did *she* really love him?

Yes. Yes, to both of those questions. She did her best to dispel her anxious thoughts.

A knock on the door prompted an answer. "Yes?"

She opened the door for Naomi. "Ruthie, are you finished? Bo is ready whenever you are."

She sucked in a breath and smiled. "I'm ready."

Bo reached for Ruth's hand under their corner table and she allowed him to grasp it. The look of love and admiration in her husband's eyes was enough to make any wife's heart melt.

She'd sensed the trepidation in his mien as they stood before the bishop taking their vows, but she suspected it wasn't from apprehension. No, his calm voice assured her of that. He'd been exacting when executing his vows and she guessed that he probably took them very seriously. No doubt, he saw their wedding as a sacred event.

Not that *she* hadn't. But this was her second marriage and because of that, it was different for her.

Somehow though, Bo's steadfastness told her that she was the only one he would ever love. It told her that no matter what trials would come upon them that he would be there by her side. It told her that she was his everything.

She sincerely hoped she would never disappoint him.

"Naomi seems happy," Bo leaned close and whispered in her ear.

"Yeah, she does. I'm glad that Olivia was able to come."

"She is your sister-in-law, right?"

"Yes. She thinks she may have met her future husband." She swallowed the sadness that threatened to dampen her mood. "I'm happy for her."

"I pray her future husband will know the joy that I

am experiencing right now." He squeezed her hand.

"I love you, Bo."

"I share your sentiments. I pray I can bring you joy all of your days."

"I don't deserve you."

"I would like to argue that point, but I'm refraining from an argument since this is our wedding day." He winked. "But I strongly disagree with your opinion."

She boldly moved her hand to his leg under the covert of their table and eyed him with a coy smile. "How long do we need to stay?"

He ducked his head and swallowed. "Just a little longer." He reached for her hand and grasped it with his own, quickly removing it from his leg.

"Good." She winked.

THIRTY-TWO

Bo yawned. The sun was already peeking over the horizon, and the rays bathed his face in warmth as he stood on the porch, promising a beautiful morning. He'd slept longer than usual, but how could he not, given his current circumstances? Circumstances he could've only dreamed he'd ever find himself in.

Who would have thought he'd have a beautiful wife? And fifteen years his junior? He shook his head in dismay. What had she seen in a man like him? He never would understand that. The Lord had been wonderful *gut* indeed. Ruthie had still been resting peacefully as he tiptoed from his bedroom. *Their bedroom.* He'd hated to leave her, but he had big plans for today and they were already set in motion.

Now he stared out the window of the breakfast nook, admiring God's handiwork. It seemed like he'd been doing a lot of that lately—admiring God's handiwork.

Last night, it had been his beautiful bride. His wife. *Wow*. He'd thought all of the air had evaporated from his lungs, making it difficult for him to breathe. His heart had seemed as though it were a horse galloping on a racetrack, vying for first place. She had snatched his breath away and left him weak as a newborn colt. Just the sight of her unabashed beauty caused him to tremble...*and her touch*, he swallowed and took a deep breath. *Jah*, she was perfect in every way.

He now understood how Adam must've felt when God presented Eve to him for the first time. No wonder Adam chose to eat the forbidden fruit. Was it possible that he couldn't bear the thought of not being with his wife? Of losing her? But, oh, if he'd had any idea of the pain and turmoil that decision would exact for millennia to come!

Bo was just glad that *he* wasn't the one required to have made that decision, because after being in his wife's arms, he wasn't sure *he* would have made the right decision either. Did women have *any* idea the power they held over men?

He'd never known the joys of marriage that he'd been missing all these years, and by the grace of God, he'd never take it for granted.

He finished off his first cup of coffee, rinsed his mug, and set it by the sink. If he was going to get anything done today, he needed to stop daydreaming.

Now, to prepare a special breakfast for his new bride. He began removing the ingredients for French toast, her favorite breakfast meal. He'd enquired of Naomi earlier and made sure to have the ingredients on hand so he could make it. Since he knew she hadn't had it in a long time, he hoped it would be a treat for her.

At the sound of footsteps, he looked up to see his wife heading in his direction. That was new too. Usually, he was alone each morning. It had been that way for years. Just him and God.

But he could get used to this.

A hint of pink splashed her cheeks as she walked into the breakfast nook. Her eyes glowed as they had last night in his arms. He drew her close and a shiver of delight tempted to distract him from the task at hand. He pressed her close to him and claimed her lips for just a few tantalizing moments. He then forced himself away, lest he become completely useless.

He cleared his throat. "I brewed some coffee and there's water for tea, if you prefer that."

"You know, you spoil me."

"I hope so." He kissed her hand. "You are a dream come true, Ruthie."

She shook her head. "I don't see how. I'm nothing special."

"Oh, but you are, my beautiful wife." He took a mug from the cupboard. "Coffee or tea?"

"Tea, please. Peppermint, if you have it."

He nodded. "I believe I do." He grinned and pulled out several boxes. "I wasn't sure what you liked, so I got a little of everything."

"See? I told you you're spoiling me."

"With sincerest pleasure, *fraa*. Now sit."

She didn't do as told. "But I need to start on breakfast."

He smiled again and shook his head. "Breakfast is my pleasure as well." He took her arm and led her to the table.

"Are you aiming to turn me into a lazy wife?"

"I'm aiming to make you a content wife."

"I already am a content wife." She pulled her bottom lip between her teeth and he found it quite becoming. As a matter of fact, everything she did was quite becoming.

"And I plan to keep you that way. Now you just relax and let me minister to you."

She laughed. "You don't need to take the 'cherish' part of our vows *this* seriously."

"On the contrary, my love. I take all my vows seriously."

"Come, *Lieb*. I have something for you." Bo called her as soon as she finished dressing after breakfast.

"For me? What could you possibly give me that I don't already possess? I have all I need right here."

He was indeed spoiling her. She'd already known that he was a kind man, but she had no idea of the depths of his love. What woman would not want to be married to him?

"Shh…you're talking too much," he teased, happy to hear a gasp from her lips. "Now close your eyes."

When she did, he took her by the hand and led her outside. "You may open them now."

She stared at the hitching post, or rather what was tied to the hitching post. Her mouth dropped open. "Is it…?"

She looked at Bo, then back at the horse. She moved closer and held her hand out. The horse dipped its head and rubbed his neck against her hand. "It is! You…you bought Timber, Mahlon's horse?" Her eyes searched her husband's as she gently stroked the stallion's neck.

He smiled. "I did. Is this a good wedding gift?"

She stepped back from Timber, stood on her tiptoes and brought Bo's lips to her own. "Oh, Bo, it's the best!

I have the kindest husband that ever lived."

He waved a hand in front of his face, promptly dismissing her comment. "Don't say such things."

"But it's true. You make so happy."

"I'm glad that I do, but you should not depend on me for your happiness. I may not always be here, and sooner or later I *will* let you down. The only person who can bring you happiness—true joy—is Jesus. He will walk with you every day. He will be there no matter what you go through. He will be there when no one else is."

"You are right, but I'm thrilled that He's blessed my life with you."

"I feel the same about you, *lieb*." He caressed her cheek, then turned back to Timber. "What would you say if we used him as a stud?"

"That's what Mahlon had always wanted to do. It's why he bought a stallion instead of a gelding."

"He must've bought him young."

"He did."

"Then we will honor your first husband by fulfilling his dreams."

"What did I ever do to be blessed with a man like you?'

"Ruthie, *you* own a beauty you'll never know."

"What does that mean?"

"It means that your beauty runs so deep, it infuses all you are and all you do. You will never see it because that's part of what it is, it's who you are." He caressed her cheek. "I wrote you a poem. Would you like to hear it?"

Ruth nodded. "I'd love to."

"Okay, I'm not a poet, so give me some slack." He warned with a chuckle.

"Ruth, my Ruthie, the sum of all beauty
The love of my life, I've made you my wife
But a wife you're not only, can you not see?
Ruthie, my love, you're the world to me

"When you entered my field, I saw you afar
You hadn't realized, you'd stolen my heart
You danced into my life, when I was alone
You gave me your heart, I gave you my home

"When you lost your first love, and you wept sore
Did you ever imagine, what God had in store?
You moved to a land, foreign but free
Did you ever imagine, what your heart might see?

"A blessing from God, as plain as day
I'd always believed, He would make a way

I was sure lonely, for a woman like you
Who knew our one, could be made from two?"

"You're amazing." Ruth leaned in close and kissed his lips. "I love you."

THIRTY-THREE

*B*o had sensed something had been bothering Ruthie for a while now. He wanted her to open up to him. He wanted her to share her heart with him. He wanted to meet her needs, satisfy her desires, calm her fears.

"Do you want to talk, *lieb*?" He prompted, reaching for her hand across the supper table, hoping she'd share her heart.

"I worry about Naomi. Especially now that we're married. I think she might feel extra lonely."

"You have such a kind, caring spirit, *lieb*. Naomi will be fine, just give her some time." He blew out a relieved breath, glad to know it wasn't something *he* was doing wrong.

"It seems like ever since Eli, Mahlon, and Leon died, she's been fighting some unseen battle. I realize the sadness and the grief that comes with losing a husband, but she has nearly given up on life and it pains me to watch her. Naomi carries around a deep bitterness in her heart. I fear she is angry with God.

"I understand what she is going through. I still have many of my own questions that haven't been answered. But I can't be angry with God. He's given me so much."

"What questions do you have?"

"Well, why Mahlon died so young. Why did God not allow me and Mahlon to have a baby? Things like that, I guess."

Bo's heart clenched. He should have known he couldn't be everything for Ruthie, but he'd hoped... Was there something he wasn't doing right? Was he not fulfilling her needs? *God, please help me. Show me.*

He shook his head. She was worried about Naomi now. She needed guidance. He'd do the best he could to offer some. "When things don't go the way we planned or the way we hoped they would, it's easy to turn bitter. We think that God is unjust because we can only see what our narrow view contains. But God, He sees it all. He knows what's best for us and He could be doing something amazing right now that we will never know this side of eternity. He might be planning some grand scheme that not only encompasses our generation, but generations in the centuries to come.

"When we hold on to bitterness, we deny ourselves the peace that comes from casting our cares on Him. We are not trusting God to know what's best. We think that our way is better than His. God wants to carry our burdens for us, but *we* have to let them go in order for Him to do that."

Ruth nodded. "Will you talk to Naomi? I think your words could help her."

"I'm sure I haven't said anything that she hasn't already heard from the bishop's mouth or from one of the ministers. I will speak with her, if that is what you wish. But let us pray that somehow God will lift her grief so she can release her bitterness."

"Yes, it would be nice to see her *really* smile again."

Bo entered the house, surprised to hear nothing but his echoing footsteps. Where was Ruthie? She'd typically be in the kitchen making candles or the hum of her sewing machine could be heard, but not today. He'd have noticed if she was on the porch. He hadn't seen her out in the field or in the arena with Timber. She wouldn't have left the house without making him aware.

His heart began to pound. Where was she? What if

something was wrong? What if she realized what a terrible mistake she'd made in marrying him, and she left? No, he would not allow fear take hold of his mind. He had no doubt that she loved him. He continued to look into each room as he passed by.

Where was she? "Ruthie?"

He walked to their bedroom and opened the door, not bothering to knock. She was…in bed? His heartbeat slowed momentarily.

He softly approached the bed and sat down on the edge. Ruthie's gentle breathing floated through the air. He placed his hand to her forehead but it hadn't indicated a fever. He leaned close and kissed her cheek. If she was tired, he would let her sleep.

He said a silent prayer, then slipped outside, leaving his concerns in God's hands.

"You slept in late this morning." Bo took a bite of the sandwich she'd prepared for his lunch.

She eyed him from across the table, but didn't hold his gaze. "*Jah.*"

"Are you…feeling okay?"

She nodded in silence.

"Ruthie, if something is wrong`

"Nothing is wrong."

"*Gut.*" He reached for her hand. "I'm glad."

Silence continued to fill the room until he couldn't stand it anymore. There may be nothing wrong, but something wasn't being said. He could sense it.

"My *fraa* is acting…different. You are not telling me something, Ruthie. I want you to be able to share anything with me. It pains me that you feel like you can't."

"I didn't want to say anything until I was sure of it. I think I *might* be in the family way."

"You…really?" His stomach flip-flopped.

She shrugged. "I didn't want to get our hopes up. If I'm not…"

"If you're not, it is perfectly okay. But if you are…" He couldn't contain his grin. "We will trust *Der Herr*, okay? This is not something to worry about."

"No, it's not."

"You rest as much as you need to, *fraa*. And don't overdo it."

"Bo…" She frowned.

"Husband's orders." He kissed her forehead before he slipped outside, whistling as he went on his way. *Gott, I would not be disappointed in the least if You wanted to give Ruthie and me a child. I will do my best to raise him to know You and serve You with all his heart.*

"If we have a boy, I'd like to name him after your first husband, to honor him."

Ruth's heart warmed at Bo's pronouncement. "Oh, Bo! Are you sure? You'd...do that for him?"

"For him and for you, *jah*."

"I don't know what to say."

"Just say you love me. That's all I need to hear."

She moved close and, without hesitation, reached behind his neck and pulled his lips to hers. "Bo King, I love you more than life itself."

EPILOGUE

"Naomi, it's time!" Bo hollered from the door of his and Ruthie's bedroom.

"You should probably go now," Ruth managed between labored breaths.

"There's no way I'm leaving you alone, *lieb*." He poked his head out and called for his mother-in-law again.

Ruthie panted hard. "Is she coming?!"

"I don't know." He moved from the door and came to his wife's side.

"I need to push now!"

Bo's heart raced. "Where could she be?"

"I don't know!" Ruthie bore down, her hands desperately gripping the blanket over her, and her face turning several shades of red.

"I…" There was no time for indecision. He had to help his wife. He pulled one of the stacked towels from the dresser and moved into the midwife's position. "Okay. I'm ready."

Ruthie pushed again, and Bo witnessed the head of his posterity crowning. His heart pounded. "You're doing good, *lieb*. I can see him."

Two more pushes and the *boppli* slipped from Ruthie's womb and into his hands, which shook with sheer wonder and amazement.

"Our *boppli*. It's a *maedel*! We have a girl, Ruthie."

The baby's cry met their ears and joy filled Bo's heart. God had been so good!

"Bo! What are you doing in here?" Naomi's alarmed voice called as she dashed through the door.

"I called for you but you didn't come. Meet your *grossdochder*!"

"*Geh*!" Naomi commanded.

"Just as soon as *mei fraa* sees our baby girl and gets a kiss from me." He moved to Ruthie's bedside and happily allowed Naomi to perform the remainder of the midwifery duties. He placed the tiny baby into his wife's arms. "Meet our *dochder*."

"Oh, Bo, she's beautiful!" He'd never tire of hearing the joy in Ruthie's voice, although he knew she must be exhausted.

He bent down and kissed her lips. "Just like her mama. You did *zehr gut*, *lieb*. *Gott* has given us another blessing. Now, I better get out of here before Naomi brings out the broom to paddle my backside."

Ruthie laughed. "It won't be long."

"I know. It will give me some time to thank *Der Herr*." He slipped out of the room.

Ruth smiled down at the newborn *boppli* in her arms, gazing into her innocent eyes, as her tiny hand fisted around her loose *kapp* string. What did the future hold for this little one?

"Someone else would like to see his new sister too." She hadn't even heard anyone enter the room, let alone her husband and son.

She looked up into the eyes of her beloved – the one who had saved her from widowhood and childlessness, saved her life, really. He had been so good and kind and merciful. And he was certainly the best father that ever walked the earth.

She stroked her boy's hand. "See, Mahlon? It is your *schweschder. Ein boppli.*"

The one-year-old's eyes widened as he reached for his sister's hand.

"Gentle," Bo cautioned, holding him securely in his arms.

Ruth surveyed the room. "Has Naomi gone?"

"Yes, she has left but she should return shortly. Do you need something? I could get it for you. She ordered me to make sure you get some rest." He lightly massaged her shoulder.

"No, I'm fine."

"Has the little one eaten?"

She didn't miss his look of wonder as he stared down at the precious blessing she held.

"She should have a full tummy." She kissed the *boppli's* head.

"In that case, she's all mine. You take a nap now, *lieb*. You know visitors will be stopping by and you'll need all the energy you can get. Not to mention, this little one will no doubt keep us up at night." He leaned over and kissed her lips before securing the baby in his arms. Their young daughter looked extra tiny next to her bulky father, who now radiated happiness. Having *bopplin* in his later years was no doubt excellent medicine for his heart.

It had certainly been good medicine for Naomi. Ruth hadn't seen her this happy since Eli was alive. Joy had surely returned to her mother-in-law's life. And to her own life as well.

Naomi waltzed through the door, carrying a large brightly colored bag. "I will take that little one now!" she declared.

"*Mammi!*" Young Mahlon jumped into his *grossmudder's* arms and she smothered him with kisses.

"Did you miss *Mammi?*"

He reached for the bag she held.

"You know *Mammi* bought something for you too. You are too smart." She reached into the bag and pulled out a toy truck half Mahlon's size.

He immediately sat on the floor with the toy vehicle and began making engine noises. Where had he learned that from?

Ruth gasped. "You're going to spoil him, for sure."

"Oh, there's no such thing." Naomi waved a hand in front of her face, as though swatting away a pesky fly. "Besides, what are *grossmudders* for?"

"Cookies!" Mahlon exclaimed.

They all laughed at Mahlon's interjection.

"I didn't even know he knew that word," Ruth said.

Bo handed the *boppli* to Naomi and guided Mahlon and his truck out the door. "Get some sleep now, *lieb.*"

Ruth nestled deep into the blankets under her quilt as soon as her beloved closed the door. Her eyes draped shut and she thanked *Der Herr* for lavishing such wonderful gifts upon her. When she'd thought all hope and happiness was gone, she'd had no idea that God would come along and unbreak her heart. And that was exactly what He'd done.

THE END

Thanks for reading!

To find out more about J.E.B. Spredemann, join our email list, or purchase other books, please visit us at www.jebspredemann.com. Our books are available in Paperback, eBook, and Audiobook formats. You may also follow J.E.B. Spredemann on Facebook, Pinterest, Twitter, Bookbub, Amazon, and Goodreads.

Questions and comments are always welcome. Feel free to email the author at jebspredemann@gmail.com.

Discussion Questions

1. Ruth knew very little about the Amish culture before she met Mahlon, yet she was intrigued by them. What draws you most to the Amish culture?

2. Ruth was surprised by the Amish traditions and the things they disallowed such as having wedding photos. Do you think you'd be able to abide the rules of the Amish church?

3. Mahlon knew dating Ruthie was forbidden but he chose to anyway. Do you think he ever came to regret his decision? Why or why not?

4. Do you think Ruth's father was justified in how he tried to protect his daughter? Why or why not?

5. Do you believe what Mahlon and Ruthie did was wrong? If so, how could they have gone about it a different way?

6. Death is inevitable, yet it often seems to take us by surprise. How can we prepare ourselves for the death of a loved one? For our own death?

7. Letting Timber go was difficult for Ruth, yet she knew it must be done. Have you ever had to part with something/someone dear to your heart?

8. Have you ever heard of or participated in gleaning? If so, please share your experience.

9. Bo had almost everything a man could want, yet he still lacked one thing. Have you ever been in a similar situation? Did you trust God, as Bo did, for His provision?

10. What do you think of age differences in marriage?

11. Ruth was selfless in that she was willing to do whatever it took to provide for Naomi's needs. Have you ever known a love so loyal?

12. Bo was confident with sharing the truth of God's love and salvation with Ruthie. Are you confident about sharing your faith?

13. If you're unable to answer the previous question, would you consider speaking with a pastor to learn more about the life-changing faith that Ruthie found?

A SPECIAL THANK YOU

I'd like to take this time to thank everyone that had any involvement in this book and its production, including Mom and Dad, who have always been supportive of my writing, my longsuffering Family - especially my handsome, encouraging Hubby, my former-Amish friends who have helped immensely in my understanding of the Amish ways, my supportive Pastor and Church family, my Proofreaders, my Editor, my CIA Facebook author friends who have been a tremendous help, my wonderful Readers who buy, read, offer great input, and leave encouraging reviews and emails, my awesome Street Team who, I'm confident, will 'Sprede the Word' about my books! And last, but certainly not least, I'd like to thank my **Precious LORD and SAVIOUR JESUS CHRIST**, for without Him, none of this would have been possible!